INTERNATIONAL AIRLINES

GREASED SAMBA

30.⁰⁰

V8

AIR CARGO EXPRESS

SEATTLE
PORTLAND
SFO/OAKLAND
(415) 877-8126

LOS ANGELES
CARACAS

PHOENIX
MEXICO
FORT LAUDERDALE/MIAMI
(305) 522-1555

GREASED SAMBA

AND OTHER STORIES

Also by John Deck

ONE MORNING, FOR PLEASURE

JOHN DECK

GREASED SAMBA
AND OTHER STORIES

Harcourt Brace Jovanovich, Inc.
New York

First edition

ISBN 0–15–136875–9

Library of Congress Catalog Card Number: 77–117571

Printed in the United States of America

To my mother and father

CONTENTS

THE WAY
THE WIND BLOWS

Then there was a bright June morning in 1960 and the Dillmans were bounding down a dirt road in a shadowy Sierra Nevada canyon, in a jeep driven by a portly, pleasant forest ranger. The proper place to heal all domestic ailments seemed to be just over the crest of the next hill. Sylvia Dillman was in the front seat, greedily breathing the clear air. Thomas Dillman sat behind her on a metal slat, suspended over a large box of groceries, luggage, a few kitchen utensils and blankets.

"You won't be able to see any of the famous places," Roger the ranger said. "Donner summit is north a ways. Tahoe, east. But you'll have plenty to look at. If you get lonesome you can see number seven tower."

"How close is number seven?" Sylvia asked.

"Oh, ten—fifteen miles. Like that."

"Pretty cramped," Sylvia said, smiling over her shoulder at Tom.

"Cramped?" Roger saw she was joking. He laughed generously. He had vigorous pink cheeks puffing beneath the broad brim of his hat. He wore a coarse, dark-green uniform and a look of ministerial confidence. But he was amiable, and a virtuoso jeep driver. He avoided all the larger chuckholes, spoke of the days of the gold rush, and eyed Sylvia's large breasts jostling in the loose canvas halter. These levels of concentration impressed Dillman. He felt a kinship with the ranger. Riding with him, with Sylvia safely stowed in the front seat, Dillman was serving several levels of his own concern. Spending the summer watching for forest fires struck his wife as *right*; she supported conservation. And there was the money. And distance from the familiar.

So when the jeep leaned back and the engine whined against the angle of ascent, Tom was almost smug. The trimmed row of trees cut back for the road began to thin out. Emerging from canyon shadow, he enjoyed the high-altitude air, thin and dry, and the sun's hard slap at his forehead.

"You come to the base of the hill for your water," Roger ranger said. "Pipe's down there. Tower's just over the top."

A telephone line was strung on raw poles along the fire-break. They were approaching timber line. Impoverished firs, like shrubs, dotted the leveling knoll. When they first saw the tower, Sylvia gave a little squeal.

It stood higher than the highest peak of their hill and most of those immediately surrounding—a house on metal stilts, made of aluminum, with stairs going up one side. There were windows running all around, and a railed-off cat-walk. Tanks for butane were stored among the girders. Off the edge of the grassy, dry dome, a tilting outhouse, and, beyond that, a new world.

"Jesus, will you look at that?"

"It won't be so bad, after you get used to it," Roger said.

"Bad! It's beautiful!" Sylvia stood up in the seat to look around.

"Go on up if you want a view. Tom and I'll carry up the stuff."

Sylvia jumped out and ran up the stairs, her broad buttocks lunging in the shorts, her feet strumming the metal structure. Roger ranger watched her climb, caught himself, and turned to the boxes without looking at Tom.

"Got to be careful up here. Overexertion when the air's thin. She isn't used to it." He picked up a suitcase.

They carried the supplies and luggage up, passing Sylvia's wonder, Tom's breathing already a pant. Roger unlocked the door of the cabin. Year-old odors of men and food escaped; the room was small. A counter ran under the shuttered windows, with a sink and four-burner stove inset in one corner. Two cots were rolled up on the floor. There was a metal table bolted in the center of the floor. Roger detached weatherproofing and unlatched the windows. The room suddenly extended an immense distance all ways.

"Tom, come out and look."

"We've got to unpack. And I can see from here."

"Come. Don't you care?"

He decided to care. He stepped out, Roger trailing. Sylvia was standing, the rail gripped in her hands. She nodded out toward everything without turning her head. It was a command.

Looking out, he saw all imaginable in the way of green. It spun down slopes and leaped space and scurried up cliff faces and leveled off on peaks. Where canyons dropped the green went dark to near-black shadow, and on the eastern ridges, sun-shot foliage was inlaid with gold. The top leaves of the closer, oxygen-starved trees were pale, ashy at that altitude. But it was a green place; Tom had only to look at Sylvia's fixed expression of rapture and purpose to know he'd accomplished something fine in the way of a service to their marriage.

"No one could argue with this," Sylvia said, slowly, with private emphasis.

"Argue?"

She turned to Roger. "It should be protected. It would be hell if it burned."

"Don't worry. If fire catches close by we'll drive up after you. If it's very close, we're allowed to call in helicopters. Anyway, the grass here is short. As long as the winds don't blow sheets of flame across the knoll, you're safe." Roger smiled. Sylvia turned to Dillman, her mouth indulgent.

"That isn't what I meant."

"It *should* be protected," Tom said, interpreting.

Roger straightened his shoulders in plump authority. "That's what we're here for, and if you two will come in the shack, I'll show you some of the equipment and charts." Roger turned but Sylvia stopped him.

"Where's the other tower?"

"Right over there," Roger said, lifting his forefinger toward a bit of horizon, adjusting his point a few degrees after squinting down his arm. "Can't see it from here. But you can with the glasses. Want me to show you?"

"No."

"Every evening the sun reflects off one side of it," Roger said. "I warn you so you won't think it's a fire. Most people that work this tower report the reflection as a fire before they leave."

"I doubt if we'd do that," Dillman said, following Roger

inside. He had to return for Sylvia. "Come on. Let's get rid of him."

"We can't let anything happen to this, Tom," she said.

"Come on. We won't."

Roger stayed for an hour. He made coffee, showed them maps, checked their spotting and distancing equipment, and took Dillman aside to suggest the possibility of digging a new sewer. He gave a lengthy talk of humorous anecdotes resulting from overzealousness; he soberly touched on torpor. He mentioned cabin fever as a common ailment, told them it could be avoided through the development of devices, entertainments, walks.

"I'll be up in a week with your supplies and the newspapers. And mail. You only get delivery once a week."

Dillman rode down the hill with Roger, carrying two five-gallon water cans. He filled the cans while Roger's jeep threw dust in a coiling roll off the road. The sound became a buzz and the buzz nothing in the half hour it took the climb back to the tower. Though gasping, and conscious of his clattering heart when he came up over the knoll, Dillman congratulated himself on the location, the duties, the view. He sat down on one of the cans in the slight shade of a scrubby tree, and he lit a cigarette with a proprietorial flourish. Smiling, he gazed out over his domain.

Sylvia was already scanning a quadrant with the binoculars. But she focused on him for an instant.

"Hey, you crazy bastard! Where's that match?"

He had to lift his lighter out of his shirt pocket to quiet her.

That first afternoon Sylvia took the watches. Dillman straightened up the cabin, stored their supplies, napped for an hour. He made lunch and fried a chicken for the evening meal. All perishable foods had to be consumed quickly. Roger had warned them that the last days of the week they would be eating out of cans. Dillman planned their meals after offering to relieve Sylvia again. He went back down the mountain for more water late in the afternoon. It was something to do. Sylvia's eyes were strained and rimmed with a smudge from the glasses. He felt he should be a part of her industry.

At sundown he brought paper plates out on the platform. A breeze was rustling the mountains and singing softly through the metal legs of their house. The green was gone; the sky was pale blue and some clouds strung low over a distant range were pink. It was a festive hour. Dillman handed Sylvia a drumstick.

"Fire!" She shouted, stood, pointed the chicken leg, and ran indoors. Dillman saw the brilliant patch through the dusk. He took a step inside, heard Sylvia crank the single ring for the ranger station. He thought of Roger.

"Oh . . . I'm sorry. . . . Yes, everything's fine." Sylvia stepped back out on the platform. "Roger expected the call. 'Tom or Sylvia?' he asked right away." She picked up her paper plate. "If they hadn't built these damned towers so close, they wouldn't have that trouble."

"Fifteen miles is not close."

"But I don't care," she said, pulling a bone-long strip of meat free with her teeth. She nibbled it up. "Let those stupid civil servants laugh. If I see anything—anything— I'm going to report it. This place is my responsibility. Mine."

Dillman would not deny her that. Not the first night. If she wanted it she could have it. It was his gift to her. No man could do less for the woman he loved if she was in trouble.

It had to be better than Los Angeles. Twice recently her large face, fixed in defiance, had stared at her husband from the pages of the *Times*. Before courthouse or jail, or squeezed down among the squatting congregation on the tile floors of one institution or another, Sylvia glowered under hand-painted placards demanding one freedom or decrying the loss of another. She was missing work, failing to support his laborious egress into unbiased biology—he intended to teach it, somewhere—and she had recently grown skeptical of his program for the future. She considered his ideals weak.

A large loud girl, the only child of a telephone company executive committed to money, the U.S.C. Trojans, and new Buicks, Sylvia was a mutation. As an adolescent she had memorized the songs of the Lincoln Brigade, defended J. Robert Oppenheimer before her astonished parents at their mealtimes, and cried when she could not attend summer camps sponsored by labor organizations. In college she had passed out handbills at the campus gate and besieged her professors with innumerable petitions. Dillman met her, a disgruntled veteran and part-time student, and paid court to energy, a bold vocabulary, and the young big body, so much solider than one would imagine. He won her with his clear tenor voice, harmonious with her alto on certain chants and mournful ballads of the coal fields. For a long time—for a half year of cohabitation and a year of marriage—they had known bliss.

Then she received her degree, went to work, and he quit his evening job as checker at a supermarket to study full-time. But Sylvia quickly became disgruntled. The union president really wanted a secretary, not an adviser prepared to represent the ideals of a new generation of liberals. The business manager flirted with her and was rumored to own a retreat on Catalina. A three-year contract was signed without a strike threat. And Dillman's projected career and frantic studying—he was not quick—bothered her.

She began coming to school on her lunch hour, or for whole afternoons she simply took off from her office. She was agitating. And in the whole of the Los Angeles Basin, whenever battles threatened, she marched off, a sandwich in her purse and a sneer on her lips.

"If I'm jailed *don't* bail me out!"

They had trouble talking to one another, and when talk was possible, she did most of it. Dillman listened, found himself accused of being pseudo-this and pseudo-that, a moral idler, middle-class, unsuspecting friend of the fascist, dead man. While she spoke she marched the room on great hairless calves, bosom swelling massively with her impassioned inhalations, her powerful self throwing heat like an engine held wide open. He shrank in part. And in part he was aroused.

The mountains—fire watching—had been suggested by a campus employment counselor as a summer job. Tom immediately envisioned a position of invulnerability, and Sylvia's surrender to the uncontested yet noble undertaking. He told her he was considering forestry as a major. Biology was not really a commitment.

II

Sylvia stood the main share of the watches all that week. She rose each morning before sunlight was anything more than a tentative suggestion in the east. She roused her husband to witness the rallying day. And she reported one campfire three times one afternoon. But Roger forgave her.

Not many campers kept their fires going such a long time. The second week some fishermen had their outing interrupted on her authority, and she reported the neighboring tower one morning, when the sun caught its eastern face. During the third week there was an airplane dispatched to buzz a lingering canyon mist.

Roger grinned and asked Dillman if he'd thought of a place to dig that new sewer. Dillman hadn't. They walked over to the edge of the hilltop.

"Not her fault, understand. Personally, I myself prefer watchers that work. Some people come up here and sleep all season. That pair over there for instance. Sylvia's not like that."

"No."

"If you'd just check on what she sees first."

"I do. I can't tell either."

"Then wait awhile before you call. See if it spreads."

"One of our handbooks says waiting an hour could strip acres. She's read all those handbooks, Roger. She's memorized whole pages."

"That's right." Roger agreed. "Those books were written by experts. Wait half an hour, then. See, that airplane last week, that cut into our budget."

"What'd he say?" Sylvia asked, as the jeep went out of sight.

"He said those people over there sleep all the time. And the forestry service is worried about its budget."

"He was mad because I've been calling in too often."

"But he prefers conscientious people."

"He said I was no damned good at it, didn't he? Hah?"

Sylvia had been too much in the sun. Her cheeks were covered with great flakes of dead skin and inflamed patches of delicate, scorched new stuff. And she'd quit combing her hair; it hung in uneven, knotted falls, bobbing jaggedly off her shoulders when she shook her head in agreement with her suspicions.

"Sylvia, let me take more of the watches. You rest. Read the papers or something."

He couldn't suggest she go for walks. He couldn't imagine where one would go. He devised one game. They read the week-old newspapers in chronological order, and tried to speculate on the evolution of a bit of news. But Sylvia couldn't contain herself when horrors figured in every edition; she read ahead and spoiled the diversion.

"Look what they're doing now," she'd say, coming out on the platform where Dillman watched for fire, pressing a photograph to his nose.

A dog, leaping at a throat, was caught in midspring by a chain leash. The heavy policeman in helmet looked, in profile, melancholy and uncertain, though he leaned against the dog's thwarted surge. Inches off the fangs a Negro man in overcoat and tie dodged, his hand before his face, his hat in the process of tumbling, his shoes tilted at angles that predicted a fall. Dillman looked and lingered over the picture, heeding its moment of action, sympathetic and insulted in turn. He handed the paper back.

"Horrible. The Nazi bastards."

"We should be there."

"What about this?" he said, adjusting his glasses.

"There's nothing going on."

"Wait."

Waiting they listened to the single radio station they could get clearly. It originated from one of the primitive mountain towns nearby. It was loud with commerce and the stringy, sentimental offshoots of cowboy ballads. Dill-man decided they would dance, and assured Sylvia that it was a universal and peaceful pastime. But they were both awkward and unrhythmical. The rewards were slight. Sylvia refused to sing with him.

She wore a single slip for two weeks running. She took the slip off and went naked for eight days, avoiding Roger by running off the hill when the jeep approached. Dillman said she was strolling, and Roger approved. She insisted they make love on the platform three mornings in a row. Dillman had trouble responding wholly to the desultory demands.

Abruptly she refused to share the duties. She stayed in her cot days on end. Dillman, his enlarging forehead blistering under the extended watches, had to stay indoors and peer through the opened windows. Behind him he heard Sylvia turning pages of old newspapers, wadding them up, throwing them away. He heard her groan as she got out of bed to pick them up, straighten them out to reread them, and to throw them again. The silken slip, when she donned it again, got dirtier, picking up dust and food stains and stretching to shapelessness.

"There's not going to be any fire, Tom. Come over here."

"What if it burns up?"

"There's not going to be any fire."

Roger brought up a letter from an agency that needed money to support Sylvia's interest in liberty. Sylvia wrote a check after Roger left. By the time Roger returned, the amount had tripled. Dillman destroyed it one evening. Sylvia missed it, wrote another that would have cost her what little liberty she enjoyed had it been cashed.

One evening they were eating sauerkraut and tinned wieners at the metal table. The sun was catching on the neighbors' tower. Sylvia's loose hair hung close to her paper plate, and Tom was tempted to grab it away from the steaming cabbage.

"You better comb your hair," he said.

"What for?"

"Because it looks like hell. You look like hell."

"Like a pig, hah?"

"Exactly."

"Watch," she said. She dumped the contents of her plate on the table top, and continued eating.

Dillman took the glasses and stepped outside. He scanned the immense, shadowy neighborhood, the far ridges, the pale sky. Behind the nearest tower a small cloud, pinkish brown in the sunset, hung in the soft light.

"That's smoke," he said to himself.

"Where?" Sylvia scrambled away from the table.

"There."

"Smoke? You ass. That's a cloud."

"It's brown."

"How can you be a fire watcher if you're color-blind. Give me the glasses." She stared, wheeled suddenly. "It might be," she said, gaily. She turned again. "I think it is, Tom. It is!" She laughed. "I'll call."

"Wait. It is more pink. You're right, Syl. I shouldn't be a ranger."

He saw her glee dwindle, but she remained poised. "Of course I'm right."

Dillman watched the cloud until it was too dark to see. It didn't seem to change shape, and there were no flames visible. It was beyond the close tower, out of their area. He went back into the shack, to Sylvia, combing her hair. He kissed her rough, sun-drawn cheek. She smiled.

In the morning Roger telephoned before they were awake. Sylvia took the call, then shrieked and dropped the receiver. Dillman sat up and saw that the brown cloud had become a huge destructive plume. Roger was still talking when he lifted the receiver.

". . . safe, unless the wind changes. I might be late with your stuff this week. If the wind does shift, watch for cinders."

"Right," Tom said. "We'll call you if anything happens."

"I thought I was speaking to Sylvia."

"You were. She's already watching for cinders."

"Talk to you later," Roger said.

Sylvia spent the day in the sun, watching the smoke. Three times Dillman had to hold her away from the phone.

"But we saw it first. Last night. I knew it was smoke. I *knew* it."

"They don't care. They're fighting it now. It doesn't make any difference to them."

"Then let me tell them that it looks like the wind is shifting round. It looks like the smoke is spreading south."

"They're right *there*, Syl. They know what's going on."

"We can see better from here! More!" She screamed, half-crouched, her body taut in every exposed plane. Her mouth looked torn in the set features of her face. "*I saw it! I saw it!*"

Dillman stepped to her. He took her rigid wrists in his palms and squeezed them. He squeezed until she opened her hands and looked up, straightening herself and relinquishing her rage in the slow apprehension of pain. When released, she stood still for a moment, murmuring to herself and rubbing her wrists. Then she slapped him and went to bed.

III

The fire lasted three days. On the third, the wind came round and sent smoke and bitter odors of burned timber past their tower. Dillman spent most of the day looking through the closed windows at the onrushing smoke, unable to see past the edge of their hill. Sylvia laughed at his worry. She slept and complained of the lack of food. She listened for a while to the terse commands being relayed over the telephone from spotters to fire fighters. Dillman had to stop her when she began flipping the receiver switch, interrupting the communications.

"If Roger doesn't bring us something tomorrow, I'm going to sing over it all day. I can't eat pickled beets any more. I'm sick of them."

"We only have one more can," Dillman said.

But Roger came briskly up the hill the next morning. The smoke had thinned down during the night, and carried a steamy smell of victory. Roger was brimming with praise for modern fire-fighting methods. He seemed not to notice how Sylvia had wilted; she'd ignored Dillman's request that she change out of the slip. The garment was further discolored by the day of soot. Even to Roger it could scarcely seem intimate apparel. Sylvia's anxious observations of smoke drifts were made from outside, and her face was swollen and sore.

"What caused it?"

"We think it was a couple of fishermen."

"Bastards! They should be caught and shot," Sylvia said.

"No," Roger replied. "Can't shoot 'em. Anyway, it wasn't a bad fire. Got to hand it to your neighbors. They spotted the fire early that afternoon and we were fighting it right away."

"Thought you said they were lazy?"

"Well, this is such simple work you can't hardly miss. Where there's smoke, there's fire," Roger said, lumping his wisdom. Sylvia laughed explosively.

"We've had an awful good season. Best in years." Roger walked out of the shack, up to the railing. He glanced over the unscarred surroundings with a successful proprietor's calm, as if he'd banked a better reward than anticipated.

"I've got other deliveries to make. There's steak in the box for you. It's a celebration. That fire could have been a bad one."

Dillman walked to the jeep. Roger was working his face into an embarrassed wholesomeness for a bit of prescriptive intimacy. "Sylvia looks tired, Tom."

"She's a little shaky."

"Try to convince her that we'd be up here in an instant if you were in danger."

"I will."

"See you in a week."

Sylvia screamed as the jeep dropped out of sight. She was at the door of the shack, waving the latest check she had written. The jeep engine canceled her cries, for which Dillman was thankful. Their mountain experiment had gone badly enough, and they had stayed within the limits of the law. He shrugged toward Sylvia's failure helplessly. She made an obscene gesture with her hand.

When he stepped into the cabin, he saw that she had gone through the supplies and started the steak in a skillet. Dillman went to a shelf of bottled condiments, took down the garlic salt to sprinkle it over the meat. Sylvia grabbed his hand.

"Not on mine. I want it to taste like meat."

"Choose your half, then."

"It'll spill over. I don't want garlic in the pan."

"Don't be an ass," he said, shaking his arm free.

The bottle dropped on the meat, spilling a dense semi-circle across the whole piece. Both halves would taste of garlic. Sylvia reached for the spatula and swung it at Dillman. It hit his nose, flat-on. Dillman heard and felt something soft but important break near his eyes. Blood spattered out of one nostril. He picked up the steak pan and threw the contents out an open window. The meat caught and balanced on the rail for a second, slipped over the side, leaving a bloody smear.

For a moment neither of them could move. He cupped one hand under his flowing nose and looked at Sylvia. She kept pivoting her head from rail to stove to Dillman to rail. Then she gave a brief cry and lunged at him, holding her arms out stiffly. Dillman, taken off balance, was shoved outside, unable to grasp her with his bloody hands. Sylvia darted back inside and raced about the cabin, closing and latching doors and windows. She was laughing and screaming:

"You won't ruin my food! I'll have my food my way! I'll not have it ruined! Not my food!"

Through the windows, Dillman saw his wife throw all the fresh meat into their limited number of pans and set them on the burners. She was laughing and there were smears of his blood on her forearms. She pointed at him and jeered. The room was sealed off and hot; sweat on her arms diluted his blood and made it trickle paley down toward her wrists. Sweat gathered the slip against her large body in sodden binding. Sweat glazed her face. Dillman ran down the stairs to get a rock. He would break the windows of the tower. At least she wouldn't suffocate; he could do that much.

Once on the ground he realized his nose was still spreading gore down his shirt front. And he saw the steak, dusty and under investigation by several winged bugs. He recognized his own plight and deprivation. He sat down on the bottom step, tilted his head back, and worried about his health. He heard Sylvia's thumping footsteps as she roved the cabin. Then she appeared on the top step, with a pan of meat in her hand.

"I put lots of garlic on this," she said. The half-cooked meat, a pile of ground beef and chicken parts, fell near Dillman.

"Sylvia, call the ranger station. Tell them to come and get us. There's nothing for us up here."

"Do you want some more food?" She retreated inside.

"No! Call the station. There's nothing—"

She returned to the catwalk, a wad of newspapers in her hand. "Dillman, here's something for you to do. Here's fire to fight." His cigarette lighter flashed and a wad of paper ignited. She lofted the torch over the side.

Dillman almost tripped getting at the newspaper. He had it stamped out when the next one landed. The third caught a tuft of grass but he managed to get it before it spread. Half a dozen torches followed. But both Sylvia and Tom were slow-moving in that thin air. When the cigarette lighter quit working, Sylvia had to run to the burners of the stove, which gave him a better chance. Over the hoarse heaves of his own breathing, he could hear her laughter and heavy footsteps. Before she had exhausted the week's news, her laughter gave way to gasps much like his, but thickened with sobbing.

He had no idea how long he lay in the shadow of the stubby tree. He had fallen there when he saw Sylvia's fierce face angle out over the edge of the platform, mouth broken, eyes unknowing. She was lying on the catwalk. She spoke. But he was unable to understand anything she said, and he staggered to the shade and fell unfeeling into the dust.

"I hurt myself, Dillman. Dillman, come up." That was her voice on his senses. That was what he first heard.

"My hands are burned. Tom, please."

He saw her limp hair lift in a quickening breeze. He moved his hand, then his arm, and finally he shoved his upper body off the ground. "I can't help. I can't get up."

"You have to."

He stood and walked uncertainly to the foot of the tower. He had to rest before he could climb to her. Himself a burden, he could barely care for Sylvia, even when he saw the clenched, dry, smoke-smudged fists. But he got the first-aid kit and applied an oinment to the hurt flesh. Sylvia crooned to herself while he worked. The hands were wrapped in stained gauze and left dangling at her sides when he went in to phone. He noticed that there was still a trickle of blood running freshly into the dusty clot that had dried on his shirt. It frightened him; his own welfare betrayed for her, his labors to sustain her so clearly wasted. His nose was broken and his mouth was lined with filth from the fire. The ranger could not understand what he said, and he hated repeating himself, repeating his plea.

He suggested that Sylvia wash before they were picked up. She held up her bandages. So he removed the slip and soaped her while she stood, naked and gleaming, in the sunlight on the catwalk. He went tenderly over the sunburned areas. He toweled with care. He dressed her, and she responded silently but obediently to his directions, turning as required, sitting down when asked. He brushed the tangled, filthy hair, and when his brushing had to be painful, she made no outcry.

Dillman felt better preparing her, maintaining this close, quiet communication. But when the distant roar of an approaching engine reached their peak, Sylvia started. And in that large, humbled face a wry smile appeared. Her eyes tightened defensively.

"Roger the ranger," she said. "The civil servant."

Then Dillman knew she had won. She would go down the mountain a victor. Restored forever, that freedom she deserved and he had spoiled. Leaving her alone to do her battle with the world's rampant madness was the least he could do.

"Stay right there while I wash myself," he said. She held up her bandaged hands.

THE PREFACE TO
ANONYMOUS MAX

After I beat the boy I'll stroll down to the plaza and get drunk for the first time. It will be an additional relief, boozing seriously. I'll try the local gin; I would enjoy taking it straight, or with ice alone, as Negroes and alcoholics are said to do. But I would regret becoming sick in public. I have seen people empty their stomachs on the bar, at tables, out of bus windows. You never forget the face of a person who does that. After a series of discreet triumphs, I cannot risk public display. I'll think of a suitable mix while typing this.

I am working up ardor. Nicky provides a reason every minute or two. He harasses her constantly—jerks a toy from Silly's hand, pushes her aside to get to the rocking horse, something. For weeks I have gone to bed enchanted by the prospect of beating him eventually. I believe he has become an obsession, not my first. For various reasons, which I have not time to relate now, I have let him slip away. Today, which is exactly like all the other days, I will not. My plan is to complete this, the Preface to my incredible memoirs, hurry in, wait until any offense is committed, beat him, go to the plaza and get bombed out of my skull. And it all has to be accomplished before Nicky's mother arrives to carry him off to the dentist in M——. They are scheduled to be off by one o'clock. I have almost three hours. *Bueno.*

I will call myself Max Cutley; I will say I am thirty-three years old. I am a criminal, a fugitive from justice. The police are looking for me in the United States, one of the many countries in which I do not happen to be. They are concentrating their search on the West Coast, where I once hung out. Sooner or later they will find me. I could be—men have been—killed for what I have done.

Silly shrieked just now. The palm of my right hand, my whipping hand, twitched in answer. This is what we mean by obsession. But the governess, whom I will call Miss X, is present there and will prevent serious injury. A twitch is not enough at this hour.

Nicky is a fair, handsome, thin boy of about four. His parents are American. His father is a painter, his mother a schoolteacher, as I was, once. They had lived together in this village for some months, he painting, she shopping, when a Scandinavian girl passed through and carried off the husband. I have seen her; she is gigantic. She wears filthy trousers and heavy sweaters and sandals. Her feet are huge and black with dirt; her hair is so greasy it resembles stretched strands of chewing gum. The painter and she live together in a waterless abandoned barn on a hillside down the road halfway between here and M——. They are pigs, the two of them; and I understand perfectly why they choose to live in slops.

I have Nicky in each morning as a favor to the wife, who is

trying to pack up for a return to the States. She asks me questions about crating and shipping, the strongest twine, how to pack things. I answer coldly, a yes, a no, whatever comes to mind, without the slightest pause. Having taken the law into my own hands once, I find that I have become the law in all matters.

Kidnaping is my crime. Used to be punishable by death, under the Lindbergh Law. "Their" law, not mine, of course. I have not asked for ransom, and the child is my own, Silly, so I am not certain of its application. I await their justice. *Bueno.*

There is silence now. The good Englishwoman, Miss X, is probably threatening. I will say this about her, and this alone: she is seventy years old, thin, spotted, agile, and mean as an alley cat. Here are three random samples of her "method":

"If you don't eat your breakfast, Miss Silly, your daddy will go away and never come back."

"If you don't take your bath now, your dirty toes will turn into worms in the morning."

"If you continue to cry in that way, the boo-doos will carry you off and eat you for their supper."

I don't stop these threats for two reasons: Silly is accustomed to them now; and disaster does hover over us at all times. We are not safe. I would fire the old bitch in a second, however. She could be a hundred and seventy, starving, and I'd turn her out in a second. No qualms.

It must be clear now that I don't give a damn about anything. Except Silly, at times, and my incredible life.

I will give a few hints as to the contents of my proposed autobiography. I was once extremely wealthy, successfully married (for money), and in line to inherit a profitable business. But I gave it all up, except for the child, because I had indirectly committed murder for money, and knew I would never be caught. I got bored with serenity, safety, my wife's tireless golfing. So I split the scene.

I will add a further enticement: those whom I killed were my parents.

For these reasons I have come to this quiet little town "somewhere" in southern Europe, and I have begun assembling notes toward the book which, at present, is called: *Anonymous Max*. It is, of course, only a working title. Many of the facts have to be suppressed or altered, because of the police. I will not leave myself open to incarceration. Freedom has perhaps more meaning for me than for any person who might read this.

At the same time, my obsession delights me. Perversity, sadism, madness—these attributes of the criminal do not, as some might imagine, shame him. They enlarge the meaning of freedom. I have noted somewhere the following: "Punishment would merely have extended my definition of liberty." I confess I cannot recall exactly what I meant when I wrote it; at the time I had in mind the petty thefts of childhood (taking one of all duplicate coins from my mother's purse). But I can apply it today. Punishment—jail or execution— would be perfectly in keeping with beating Nicky, not firing that tyrant of a governess, "holing up" here, in the village of N——, on this coast.

You see, I try my freedom now. I expose myself, a portion,

so that I may further value the concealed remainder. I will go farther. It is the Mediterranean coast. *Bueno.* (But don't use the Spanish as a lead; it could as well be planted.)

The rocking horse rocks furiously, so Nicky, my victim, is mounted. Silly probably watches with wonder. He is one year her senior, the only English-speaking child in N——.

Time is passing by. They have an imported tonic which others drink with their gin, but it is expensive. I cannot waste money. Perhaps a carbonated fruit juice. Miss X would know the prices.

I'll go back a bit, give the reader a taste of what will follow. I stole Silly away on a night flight. Her mother thought we were watching *The Sound of Music.* During the weeks immediately preceding our departure, I had purchased a complete wardrobe for my daughter and had her inoculated; reactions to the shots I blamed on the concessions at Disneyland. And Silly was a little soldier. I convinced her the shots were pleasant. "Look at the doctor's bright, shiny needle. He's going to give you a love pinch." She barely cried at all. I told her the clothes were being saved for her birthday. She accepted that. Of course, my ex-wife's golf helped me in all of this.

Yes, we snuck away one evening, the two of us, off to London. I had arranged for booking through to Rome; I had paid in advance. Only, by God, it would have taken some looking to find us on that flight to Rome. We were in Folkestone, waiting for a ship. Brilliant. In later chapters I'll recount our itinerary on the continent proper. It took us almost a month to get where we are. We traveled one way, got off the train, crossed the tracks, traveled back. Our arrival at

M—— was a triumph. Leaving a few bags at the station, I went out and hired a cab to drive us to C——. There I rented a hotel room, took Silly upstairs, changed her, and back we came to the desk. I swung our suitcases about wildly, asked where in C—— I could find a man who repaired suitcase locks. Once outside, I hired another cab, this one to take us to S——, where we caught a train back to M——, recovered the rest of our luggage, and came on to N——, here, by means of a public bus.

I would have given anything to see my former in-laws during that period. "Cousin" Art Cutley and sour old Winnie, with her huge face seared by golf, are big and tan, and go about in their leisure wearing shorts and white canvas sneakers. No socks, although Winnie's ankles are blue with broken blood vessels, and Art's shins are scarred. Football scars, he'll tell you, if you give him the chance. They must have been braying like asses. They are both idiots.

Silly's mother, my former wife, has only one reaction now. She snorts, shakes her head, and reaches for her putter. She lines up her feet and pokes at an imaginary ball. Sometimes the putter is make-believe as well.

There has been nothing but silence for fifteen minutes. I will go in and see what is happening.

Nothing. Miss X is reading to them. The children listen. Nicky looks particularly good today, because he's off to the dentist. He's clean, in other words. His shoes are shined. I can picture his mother pressing his short pants and shining those shoes, all alone in what was once a studio and a home. Poor. Bereft. I find it rather delightful.

By the way, she thinks I'm a widower. All do here, including Miss X. I stay to myself because of my distress. People, when drunk, are continually coming up to me and saying: "God, old man, it's awful about the wife. What a terrible thing for the child." I affect a lugubrious expression and say nothing, nod leadenly. Soon they drift away, shaking their heads.

It has been great fun. Every bit of it. Worth all. An amazing criminal "getaway."

The boy just came out on his way to the potty. I told him to aim carefully and flush afterward. He shook his head, stared at me for a moment, wistfully. I suppose he wants a father, envies Silly. I don't care. If he wants a father, he'll get a stern substitute in a little while. A walloping. I feel I must, and I will.

Bueno. But if I had perfected this I would not need provocation. I would equal Miss X, the automatic bitch. I would beat first. That sort of spontaneity takes years to develop.

For instance, when I knew my parents were dead, and that I was somewhat responsible but completely safe, according to the law, I feigned deep mourning for almost a year. I had to assimilate the guilt. That I destroyed my marriage, ruined my opportunity with "Cousin" Art made no difference to me. But I had to prepare myself for what lay ahead. I had to convince everyone that I was mad. So I stayed in bed most of the time, wearing an old yellow dressing robe of my father's, with the blinds drawn and the insurance checks under my pillow. Silly was just learning to walk then. The way the remaining Cutleys worked on that poor child, using her as a lure, is a disgrace to the name. "Max, come in and see Silly run." "Max, Silly just said: 'Dada.' Maybe she'll say it again if you'll come in and tuck her into bed." I wanted to go, but I stayed away, for the effect. And often now I regret that it was not *perfectly* in keeping with my character—my remaining in bed.

I was just laughing, to myself. In the book I'll devote several paragraphs to those days when Art marshaled his salesmen and mechanics and sent them to save me. "How's it going, keed?" they'd ask and come stumbling into the darkened bedroom. The air was never fresh; I kept it unfresh for my purposes. "When're you getting in the check pool again? We miss the hell out of you at the shop."

Art blew up one day. He came storming in while I was again adding up the money. Cheryl was off on the fairways, conveniently. Silly was napping. "What the hell is going on?" he screamed. He looked shocked. And it had been going on for about six months by then. "I loved Tim and Evelyn as much as anyone. But, by God, Max, you're head of a house now. Soon to take over one of the hottest franchises in Southern California. It's waiting out there for you to pick up, boy. You can't mope like this."

I had a punch ready for him: "I killed them, Art."

Screaming. I go.

Nicky. Little Silly, sweet as you please, clonked him with a wooden block. I went to get him something, a glass of juice, and realized that the carbonated orange drink is the proper thing to drink with gin. Screwdriver, I believe they call it.

She hid that block behind her, Miss X said, and just popped him. It's in the blood.

Back to Art. He scoffed, listened to my "theory," and left.

But I prove it, in the book. All of this will be much more detailed and our characters will emerge more clearly. If my plans hold up. And the notes I have are sharper, more pungent, than these teasers. There are portions written in the method known as "stream of consciousness." No ordinary narrative method could properly convey the experiences I have had.

My wife could be developed here a little more. She is really an enormous woman from the waist down. From Art she got hips and thighs no father would want to see on his daughter. (Silly is built like me.) She is pretty, though freckles cease being cute at a certain age; her shoulders are delicate; her breasts spritely little things.

Our wedding was dominated by those thighs. Her mincing step in the dress fooled no one. Art's beaming face and Winnie's tearless crying were in celebration of the Great Thigh Nuptials. Afterward, at the reception, a dozen of her sorority sisters filed by me, each assuring me that I had married a "good head." Cheryl had been loved because the thighs kept her home a lot. She took calls for absent sisters, lied about their jiltings, flattered the students of dentistry and engineering who would make them such wonderful husbands later. (When golf replaced me in her affections, the additional weight helped her off the tees.)

After the wedding we spent two months in Europe. It was near the end of summer. While we were gone someone else took my classes in history at the high school, and when we returned the new models were selling like mad. ("Cousin" Art Cutley owns what we call the Ford franchise in my home town.) It was during that trip that I saw N—— for the first time.

There is more to her than the hams. After she finished college she slipped out of Southern California before she became the eternal bridesmaid. Went off to New York City. Three years later she returned, a heavy ruin. She had not lost an ounce except in her face, and that had never been full. Suddenly, however, the clan was holding dinners every time a holiday came up. And I, the bachelor, found myself seated next to her. One birthday of mine, which I was celebrating with my parents at home, was interrupted by the arrival of all the Cutleys. Champagne, a cake ("Cherry baked it," Winnie whispered), and presents of all sorts. And Art's baritone lifted in "Happy Birthday." Cheryl served me, smiled, brought me another napkin when mine dropped, grinned, knelt before me to pick up the original, skirt straining mightily against the bulk of her.

My father, who hated the successful relative, said: "They're up to something." My mother said: "Let them be." And I did. Our being distant cousins delighted all.

I never found out what happened to her in New York. There was some sort of love affair, but it could have been any sort. In all the time we were together she slipped only once, mentioned a trip to the Virgin Islands during the carnival. "We loved it," she said. "We? Who're we?" She didn't answer. I have evidence to support my opinion that she lived with a Negro dope addict who was either a professional dancer or an architect. If the former, I cannot be sure whether the lover was male or female. The whole New York "question" will be thoroughly discussed. It should be one of the highlights of the book.

I just checked the time. Getting late. Forty minutes remaining at the most.

For me, in all this, there was money and respect. And pleasure. Imagine the prospect of taking over the Ford dealership. Including the used-car lot, the business took up an entire block along the main boulevard in our town. Paint out Art, paint in Max. I will try later to re-create the afternoons I spent speeding around, flat on my back on a gocart, shooting beneath the automobiles to watch the mechanics. By the time I was finished with maintenance, I could adjust any brakes, complete a minor tune-up, replace muffler–tail pipe assemblies. I worked, and I felt a great sense of accomplishment at the end of the day, when the boys gathered in the washroom and we'd all clean our hands with that ammoniacal cleanser and "shoot the shit." The happiest days of my working life. The younger men envied me, of course. Still, I insisted they call me Max, and when there was a special job that kept us overtime, I would trot out and buy beer. And I wouldn't accept a cent in repayment.

Of course, I hated sales training. Parts shops I didn't mind.

That's about it. If, in reading this over, you detect that I was being "used," rest assured that I too comprehended the scheme, watched it with much amusement. There is reason to believe that Cheryl came back from New York threatening self-mutilation (the hulking thighs); I suppose in this respect I saved her. But with "tongue in cheek."

I'm almost on my way in now, to get Nicky. Mad. *Mad!*

My youth was miserable, as you will see, but I remained quiet. Like another California criminal, I developed slowly. (I am thinking here of the young man "Rattlesnake" Dick Barker. But if I were to pick an ideal from that era and territory, I would choose Juan Soto, a consummate sonofabitch. I suppose I bear some resemblance to the PO-8, but I consider him too sweet.)

My time must be about up. There is noise from the nursery, the sounds of play, and it has been growing steadily louder. If I wait a few more minutes, it will culminate in a scream. Always does.

The one item of great interest, which I have scarcely mentioned, is the parricide. I cannot give everything away here. I will say that my father never cared much for me. He was one of those self-made men you never hear about because the job they did was mediocre. My mother brought me up in recognition of this fact. She was sure that his failure would lead him to die first, so that she would be a poor widow. She bought insurance; they were "insurance poor."

A theory of inherent weakness was transmitted to me early in childhood. My youth was miserable.

She will be here in a minute, the mother, and still I sit writing, reflecting, awaiting my fury.

The murders seem to be accidents. Only a full presentation of the case would convince anyone. I have studied the reports at length. The thickness of the ice, the distance of the skid, traffic conditions that night. There's no doubt.

Screams. I go.

The odious, conniving, dismal little sneak! His pants were covered with rivets. And he had some hard object in his back pocket, perhaps a hunting knife. Or a stone. I almost broke my hand, can hardly hold my pen. He didn't cry. Two swats and I was wounded. Silly, however, shrieked. Because I jerked him away too roughly, shouted. He was flipping her with his forefinger, had already started her howling.

Still, I beat him. Miss X had a properly surprised expression. I had better clear out now, in case the mother comes. He's certain to tell her.

I have left the house. I am on the plaza. I brought along the journal and pen. I am drinking gin with the carbonated orange drink. Too sweet. And I'm afraid to go back to sweet vermouth and soda. Mixing is always tricky business. I write a line or two, then hold my hand on the cold glass. It's swelling, I believe.

Oh, I beat him. The insanity was there. I was uncontrollable. But I'm not satisfied. The urge to show contempt is even greater now. Crimes of passion I will not commit. Crimes of contempt are for me.

A bastard of a boy his age should not be allowed to carry knives.

Perhaps I should hold back on the autobiography until I've done something more spectacular. But, as in the cases of Juan Soto and Black Bart, there may be a Harry Morse at my back right now, to end the spree before I have hit my stride.

They were on their way to Lake Tahoe one Saturday night. It was winter. The roads over the hill to Bakersfield were iced up. He, who had never received a single traffic ticket in forty years of driving, was traveling at sixty miles an hour! There can be only one reason: they were arguing. They had only one thing to argue about: their son.

I will dramatize the spat. I know exactly what I had done to enrage and disgust him. And her defense would have been the old one: "If Max is bad he got it from you." I believe this scene will be among the most brilliant in the book. It could be made into a movie, though I can't think any American producer would have the guts to tackle it.

All of it is indeed fantastic. All I've written here are just chips off the diamond. This can't be expected to convey all the intricacies, squalor, contained violence, explosive emotions that have made up a great portion of my life.

And there's more to come! There's reason to hold off awhile.

I sit here. The plaza is empty. I have a table to myself. It is quiet. But the lull is portentous. I feel as Marshal Ney might have felt, that afternoon when his few remaining troops were crossing the Dnieper at the iced-up bend. Kutuzov at his heels. The ice dangerous. The dreary prospect of continued retreat ahead—retreat with honor, of course.

But Ney could not freeze water; by himself he could not round up strays enough to assemble a force. He had exhausted himself getting where he was. So he sat down on the frozen embankment. And he went to sleep.

I'm not a Ney—no—but there is much behind me and all of it fantastic, and it has been exhausting. I need rest, repose. What interests me most is what awaits me. Forces— my private Platov—assemble across the river. I will rest in N——, store up for the attack. And when it is finished I will write these memoirs.

I've tried the gin again. Not so bad if you swallow quickly, and immediately take a drag from your cigarette. A waiter with bad teeth stands about a yard off my right elbow. He watches me write in this journal. I wonder what he is thinking.

I wonder if I am like a figure out of a newspaper story or a moving picture to him. (They have movies here.) A thin, quiet figure, carefully dressed, drinking steadily, lighting and casting away cigarettes. My face, unlike those of the other foreigners, is very pale. I can't swim; I refuse to sun-bathe.

Odd, that man, the waiter must be thinking.

Bueno.

SEQUENCE FOR
A SEAMAN

You are between thirty and forty, but you feel much older;
and you are a husband and a father, but the magnitude of
the roles, so burdensome, so infinite, has become unbearable.
Yet, as a contracted lover, as a male of iron honor and pride,
you know there is no escape. Cigarettes are killing you; your
children hear you coughing and cover their ears to block out
the scuffing sound, which probably reminds them (they are
not stupid) of a gravedigger's spadework. Your wife knows
what a mess you make of your occupation, knows to the
penny how poor you are, and she paces and frets within the
circular prison of the marriage; she seems to have forgotten
everything except the measurements of the cage. Your affection is water and weak soup; she must dream of, must crave,
the raw joints of game still hot from the kill. Yet her expres-
sions, and those of the children, are never resentful. They
are only disappointedly surprised. What? they seem to say.
Still less than yesterday? Still less than this morning?

Then you have a break, the first in years. You hear a story

at a dinner party, told by a cold, flabby, boozed-up babe—
she's older than you, a lot. Her neck is crumbling, and on
her hands she wears a pair of loose-fitting freckled gloves.
Five minutes next to her and you are convinced you would
rather be blinded on the spot than even glance at her ankles.
Discolored sacs half-full of a seeping faded ink hang beneath her eyes. You have learned from fiction that once she
was beautiful. You find it hard to believe. Then she has this
story to tell drunkenly, and you can't forget it. Days pass.
Her name is eradicated from memory. But the story prints
itself on film, and the film keeps turning:

*I was married to an importer. He was much older than I
was, and he was a generous man, worried that I would feel
I was wasting my youth on him. Once, when we were living
in the East, we decided I should go off for a while by myself,
sail somewhere.*

It is as if the houselights were already dimmed, as if
you'd been waiting for this show for months. Just as soon as
the first images appear, you see that the woman looks exactly
like Jeanne Moreau.

The husband, feeble in a robe, sits at a wrought-iron table
on a terrace. The table top is glass. Through it you can see
his feet and ankles—rigid, knobby, lifeless—like the scroll
of a cheap violin. The skin hammocks between the meta-
carpal bones of his hands. He reaches for weak tea. He
breathes with the sound of the surf tossing and drawing back
the shingle.

Feminine, as desperately whimsical as Jeanne Moreau, the
woman is seated yards away on the lawn, in a wrought-iron
chair that matches the table. A light wrap has been thrown
over her shoulders. She wears sunglasses, though it is dusk.

What is she looking at? The man who should be dead. She thinks aloud:

—Last week he caught a simple cold and today he still has it. Can a simple cold debilitate my husband? Only if I am not the person I think I am—neither the wife nor the woman.

A second woman and a powerful, squat Oriental man appear on the terrace. The woman is her sister, the man her sister's current lover (a Japanese psychiatrist with a black belt in judo).

—Oh, my sister's come to haunt me.

True. She is blonde, younger. Her legs are bare, brown, oiled. She wears spiked heels which stick in the soft grass. She tosses her head; she swings her handbag; she smiles. Every gesture is in praise of freedom, an invitation to adopt her makeshift morality, to elevate pleasure from its position as a side effect of striving to the primacy of a goal.

—You look as if you just crawled out of a murderous accident unharmed, the sister says.

—He got out too, the woman says.

—Surely you don't begrudge him that? You know that at some time we all have to start fighting only for survival. You won't be able to share in those victories of his. They are personal.

—I'm in it too. I'm surviving. Barely.

—Not the same, Barbara. He is satisfied. For him being alive is enough. For you it isn't. You should leave him for a while. Before you begin to hate him, and have to leave him forever—and leave the girls.

The dialogue is necessarily stilted, a poor translation, for its dislocating effect. You are not satisfied with the name

Barbara. But the woman continues to resemble Jeanne Moreau.

You arrange the next scene carefully. Four beautiful daughters, ages ranging from six to sixteen, are occupied in a large room which is full of light, large pillows, thick, colorful Scandinavian rugs with stark designs. The youngest girl is reading, the oldest is seated in a lotus position, palms cupped over her knees, forefingers and thumbs touching, forming a circle. She meditates. The two remaining girls, twins, paint on panes of clear glass. Your camera lingers on the twins and their painting. The blondeness of the girls, the richness of the color, which is not stopped by canvas but splashes wetly against every fixture in the large room. When the paintings are done, the two panes of glass are moved together to produce a single startling effect. It is beautiful.

In her first vulgar gesture, Barbara scratches her scalp. It is the sound of a fingernail scraping along the teeth of a comb.

—I'm . . . I may be going away.

—We'll come and say good-bye as soon as we've finished, one of the twins says.

And the others—all but the meditator—nod.

Barbara waits, starts to form words, to say more. But she doesn't. These children are complete, content, applied. *She is not needed.*

The final domestic scene: you move on to the bedroom. The husband, still in his robe, slumps in his chair. There is a pamphlet printed in an Oriental language fallen to the floor beneath a thin hand. His face is a tragedy; broken veins, huge pores, wrinkles. It is a lunar landscape. That is how you show it: the lunar landscape, then the face, then the slumped man. He could be dead.

Barbara thinks he is dead. She removes her glasses for the first time.

—Has it finally happened? she whispers. Are you dead?

She moves forward, sadness registering in a fold on the brow, a tremor on her chin, a spastic tucking of the lip.

—Lewis, are you dead? Hoarsely, louder.

—Unnhh? Hmmmm? Wa? Wha? He shudders, jerks, blinks. He yawns, and there is a gummy, chewing sound to accompany the yawn.

She puts the glasses on. —I thought you were dead.

—Did you want me to be dead?

—Not when I thought you were, no.

He looks up, smiles. He is not such a bad old man. He has given her everything he can. It isn't his fault that he's old. He has given her daughters, the terrace, the glasses, the wrap. You want this scene to convey his devotion and decency.

—You must be very tired of me. Sick, wheezing, weak old man. And the girls all act like women now. They've become independent. Your house runs itself. The girls learn, the husband forgets, and the house goes on by itself. What is there for you here?

—You've been talking to my sister. She says I should travel for a while.

—No, I haven't spoken to her, but she's right. You should go away. You should go by choice, now. He pauses, considers. Before you are driven away. Let me think, do I know of any ships? There must be some taking cargo down to the islands. . . . Hand me the telephone, dear.

Fade-out.

I booked passage on a small white freighter, which de-

livered textiles, automobiles, things like that, to the South Pacific. She tramped between the islands after she had delivered her cargo. Imagine how I felt when I discovered I was the only passenger.

The husband is far too weak to climb the gangway. The daughters repectfully remain at his side. You show Barbara and her sister, followed by men bearing luggage, against a background of helmeted longshoremen, cranes, forklifts, dollies, crates, long shed with gaping doors. We hear the engines whine, see small cars in nets lifted off the dock. As for your ship, you keep it hidden, tease us with it. It is beautiful.

They pause in an open passageway. The sister looks about her. —It's a silly little ship, but I brought you a crate of liquor. You can stay drunk for a month.

There is some concern with the number of Barbara's cabin. And no one comes to meet her. What is that number? The sister can't remember. She will find someone who knows. She has no sooner walked off the picture frame than a steward, a Jamaican black man, and an Oriental sailor appear at Barbara's side.

—The missus can have any cabin, says the steward, but the best is number three.

—No stinkee from fool, says the sailor, in what you hope will be a comic accent.

—What?

—There is no fuel smell. None of the cabins are at all bad, but this is free of the smell entirely.

—Why isn't it reserved?

—No other body swim, says the sailor. (You try again for comedy.)

—What?

—You are the only passenger.

Barbara's eyes widen. The only passenger? Hasn't she been lonely enough all these years? She looks down at her family, a suggestion of regret in her face.

But the Jamaican steward, the sailor, and other crewmen, whose heads appear from other levels, from portholes, from around the corners, are all looking lustfully at Barbara. Her breasts, the pink skin behind her knees, her neck, her flaring matronly hips. This scene you include in preparation for your own entry.

She is guided to the cabin. It is all white except for a reproduction of Gauguin's "Otahi." Barbara looks long at the crouching woman on knees and elbows; why are her knees so wide apart, why those hands propping the head? Why are her breasts lighter than her back? Why does that cloth covering her buttocks look less like clothing, more like something tossed over her for quick concealment? Does it look like that?

—This is a very bright cabin, she remarks.

—This is a very bright ship, says the steward.

And now you show your ship for the first time. From a hundred angles. Quickly. It is all white. The winches are white, the cables are white, the anchor chain white, the covers on the lifeboats, the plates, the hatch covers. Peer into a vent and the shadow is white. The sand in the fire buckets is as white as the steam from the stacks. Everything white. It is the whitest, brightest small freighter in maritime history. You give us a look in at the paint locker: can after can after can of white paint.

Then you cut to the black bottles of liquor in the crate. The wrappings and foil.

—Bill won't like that, missus, says the steward. You're expected to use our drink.

—Who's Bill?

—Matter, says the Oriental, his accent now serving to point your meaning.

—The matter?

—The master. I call him Bill. But no one else does. You'll have to call him Master. Or Captain. Bill's an American, you see. Ashamed. That's the kind of fellow he is.

—He number-one fine matter.

Suddenly the sister comes to the cabin. She is excited. Smiling.

—God, if I could get the shots and had a ticket, I'd come right along with you. I would. I'd drop Yamaguchi in a second, despite his black belt in judo.

—Why?

—I've just seen the captain.

She's just seen you!

The ship leaves the port, goes out unassisted by tugs, but goes out astern. You take her out, after noting current from astern, holding the after bow spring and easing out on the quarter breast, watching her swing out.

You are up above Barbara somewhere. Perhaps you're seen as a shoulder of a blue coat, a hat, a face obscured by cupped hand.

—Cast off all line! you shout. We're clear, Mister Gresham! Take her on out!

Barbara is seen from the dock. She is waving a white scarf. The ship turns slowly, comes round to make headway. Nothing is visible of Barbara but the scarf as the superstructure of the vessel comes between her and the people on the wharf.

You are worried about the nautical language, the terms.

But it is too late to worry about that, isn't it? You have already set sail in this. The sea show has begun.

The master didn't come out of his cabin for a day or two. I didn't even know who he was.

You remain to yourself, in the manner of Ahab, but you never say why—not to her, not to your officers, not to the crew, not quite to Harvey, not quite to yourself. It is not for reasons of an expected emergency. For the master, even Typhoon Betsy, now taking shape off the Philippines, is not an emergency. It is merely a different kind of weather, requiring a different form of leadership. Leaving ports for the last six or seven trips, you have felt you would better serve crew, ship, and owners by remaining in your cabin.

You have worked over your charts, checked and rechecked your cargo. You have thought about the men, their watch assignments, the length of time between ports of call, the bother with this storm. Well, it won't be as bad as that trip you made to the New Hebrides, when you had the deck cargo aboard. Earth-moving equipment for some construction job, lashed down, but damned chancy, and then that wind.

Perhaps this woman will bring you luck. You still look for signs, and a pretty woman aboard can be good or bad luck. Gresham, your dapper, handsome young first officer will be trying to sound her out. Harvey and you have already had some laughs about Gresham racing across the dining room to her with his cigarette lighter coming before him, like an Olympic torch. When there are women aboard, he affects his turtleneck sweaters, and some of the crew call him "Mr. U-boat." He's a school sailor, out of some maritime institute. Rich family with shipping interests. You are a Scandinavian (not an American), probably a Swede (Max von Sydow), and you shipped out for the first time when you were eleven. Now you are fifty, lank, with your head almost shaved and your beard trimmed, and a strange occurrence—a repeated pain—which keeps you in the cabin when you leave port. No, paper work keeps you in, and the pain makes the quiet and inactivity less bothersome.

You don't even notice it until the third evening out; Harvey comes in and tells you that, when he straightened up her cabin that afternoon, he noticed that one of the brandy bottles had been opened and that two glasses had been used. Gresham making his rounds. So you decide that night you'll go down for the meal. You never cared much for that part of it—for introducing yourself to passengers. Isn't that why you've avoided shipping aboard liners for all these years?

You bring the camera up close when you have showered, dressed, cleaned your teeth, knotted and reknotted the tie, decided against the monocle again (you always do, though you need it). You are putting on your hat when the twinge hits—it's as if your sternum were a metal blade and something touched it, plucked it and set it vibrating. Your hands with the hat in them pause above your head. Your breath catches. Uhhh! The vibrations diminish. You put the hat on. Lean forward, peer at the long face, the gigantic jaw. Your eyes are clear. Your nostrils are distended, bloodless white as a reaction to the twinge. That's bad. You didn't know there were detectable signs. The sea argues against dissembling—it is the privacy accorded to the master. Have you been fooling yourself? Forget it.

Think about the woman. Harvey's reports about her whisky and innumerable gowns, pairs of slippers, assortment of cosmetics. You know her, then. You have sailed with her before. You will have that silly worry to contend with, that notion that you might forget her name, call her Olga, or Jennifer, or Aurelia, or another of the names of the many women who have shipped with you.

You don't realize what it means to be a master.

When you walk into the dining room, Gresham's young, handsome face collapses into the angleless and unattractive arrangement devised by envy. He stands. The woman—what is it again, Barbara?—turns to look at you. She stares, glances at Gresham, turns again to you. Gresham excuses himself, first to you, then to the lady, a dismal lapse of romanticism that will probably cause him anxiety later.

—Thank you, Mr. Gresham, for looking after our guest.

In the corner of your eye you see the other officers hide their grins, turn abruptly to their food, shoulders heaving mirthfully.

Barbara has changed subtly since you first invented her. She looks less like Jeanne Moreau now. She too is Scandinavian. She has more color, and her hair has dried out, thickened, brightened under your sun, in the glare of your ship, your sea. She wears earrings and a bracelet. For the first time you have fixed her with jewels. You recall the wanton regard of her sister, when she came aboard.

—I am the master of this ship.

—I thought . . . I . . .

—May I sit down? You thought Mr. Gresham was the captain of this small white freighter. I'm afraid he does almost nothing to convince our passengers otherwise. I should have asked Harvey, the steward, to tell you that I, like Ahab, remain in my cabin.

You wait, a faint tremor of expectancy freeing your features.

—Are we looking for whales?

Ah, she is better than most. You smile.

—No. Unhappily, we are in pursuit of commerce. But you needn't bother yourself with that. You can rest.

You wait again. Will she deny that she wants rest? Will she allude to the probable onslaught of boredom?

—I'll sail day by day. I'll float. I am tired of the land. Very tired.

It is time to flatter your guest. —You will be a good traveler, part of the crew before you know it.

It was the first and last time in my life that I felt I had nothing to do with what happened to me. Not that he was irresistible, but I had no reason to resist. I felt safe.

You give her the extensive tour of the ship after dinner. You must make her feel safe. You show her the bridge, the chartroom, the radarscope. You show her the gyrocompass; you speak of the superiority of that compass, the effect of the gimbal rings, the three axes: vertical, horizontal, and spinning. You show her how it is powered and how batteries are kept as auxiliaries. You also indicate that there is a common magnetic compass aboard. You show her the nav table, the azimuth rings, the Loran scope, the sextant. You ask permission of your helmsman to allow her to steer the ship.

—Sorry, Captain, but it is against policy, he says, stiffly, his lesson learned.

Your rule, long since laid down, to keep the passengers out of the pilothouse when they get bored.

You take her down to the engine room, where she immediately recognizes Wong Lee, and nods. (You had him put on this watch this night, especially, so that she would see him, and he would nod.) You do not discuss the engines with her. Let her listen to the roar. She sees the shafts twisting, the piston arms rising, the dials holding steady. A passenger does not associate the master with the machinery except in times of emergency. Let her meet the cheerful, sweating Charlie Blackshire, a short pudgy mech with boiled skin. No problems.

On the main deck you haul back a hatch cover, and with an Aldis lamp you prove to Barbara that the rice sacks are dry, that the refrigerators, television sets, air-conditioning units, and washing machines are riding smoothly. Show her the automobiles, secured fast, covered with rust-resistant protective coat, huddled close together in the gloom, like a litter of machinery warm and snug in the ship's womb.

Safe.

Everything safe.

You see her to her cabin. She stops at the door. Her eyes fumble with several notions, some quite unladylike; she becomes a sailor quickly.

—Come in for brandy?

—Yes.

You remove your hat only; even though the tropics have asserted themselves, you never remove your coat until you have taken a woman several times, at least a half-dozen. This because of the buttons: they are heavy brass buttons with anchors embossed on them. You lie upon her and the weight of your body presses the anchors into her flesh. The impressions are at first merely physical, therefore transitory. But after several sessions, they remain. You know she will never be rid of them.

You have had letters from women you knew when you were a third mate on a different ship in another ocean. They all say they are still "wearing your buttons" years later. None complain. You throw the letters out after reading them per-functorily.

I couldn't stop him.

She can't stop you. She doesn't try.

You know that the things you do to her cannot be photo-graphed, so you do not bother to enumerate them, not even to yourself. At times she is frantic; at times she sobs; at times she acts as if she were bruised from head to foot. Most of the time she pours your glass of brandy first thing in the morning, and Harvey has to beg her to come to the dining room.

She becomes, as they all do, a part of the ship's routine. Each day you inspect your ship, look for rust, check the bilges, listen to the weather report, visit Barbara, chart your location, converse with your officers, and so forth. You cannot stay away from her. You would be neglecting your duty, forgetting responsibilities, betraying the owners. Yes, you admit you would also be degrading this part-time, paying crew member. And you like her. She has spirit.

You must teach her things. You must tell her about the Mariana Trench, the sweet winds blowing from the horse latitudes to the doldrums; why nylon rope, though in many ways better than fiber, inspires too much faith in the sailors, and hence the terrible accidents when the line parts with the resultant pistol-loud, dangerous snapback.

You tell her about the smells of islands, of vanilla and copra, of rotting cane, of fish and food, of the sickening stench of a mandrake swamp or bêche-de-mer. All the books you have ever read about the Pacific have smells in them, and as master you know they are correct. You must prepare her for the port, prepare her senses, her perceptions. You must tell her of the people, the weird rites, the tabu huts, the attitudes of traders, the sexual liberties, the languor of the people.

So much to say, day by day, as Typhoon Betsy heads north and you sail south, in luck again. Never neglect a good woman, Bill, you tell yourself. And twice before you reach the first stop, the twinge on the sternum reminds you that, after this port, you must stay in the cabin, get the paper work caught up, tend to your ship's log. You are prompted to remember.

It started off as a month's cruise, but with the chance that he would pick up cargo along the way. We were gone three months. I can't remember which islands we stopped at. They looked the same to me.

You pick up copra. You pick up all the equipment for a missionary hospital. You leave rice, seven Toyotas, two refrigerators. Your chest hurts. So . . .

You stay in your cabin one day and one night, working like hell, and when your chest hurts, you think: Damn it all, I'll get the work done. I've never failed yet, never lost a ship or a man.

The twinge deepens and drops. It deserts the bone, plunges into the flesh. It slithers, like a coral worm, down toward the heart. Twice you are tempted to take down your medical encyclopedia—for you are master medico as well— but you don't. No. You're a superstitious fool, true: you hate a ring around the moon, a cat on board, three upright marching cumulus soldiers at sundown. But superstition is just a way of fighting the boredom of the seas. It is entertainment for a master. But whimper once, let the word get around that the skipper trembled, and the sailors falter. You become a sign for them; a way to quicken their superstitiousness. And they are like children, every man jack one of them. For them the sign is not antidote to sameness. It is fact pronounced in a foreign language. When a captain sneezes, the bowels of the ship open up, the engines develop strange noises, the typhoon changes direction, the compasses are skewed.

You know this when Harvey catches you once with the blood drained from your nostrils and an "O" stopped at the portals of the mouth, just before it becomes sound.

—What is it, Billy?

—Little catch in the chest. No use trying to fool Harvey, so you tell him.

—Mind if I give it a listen?

You consent. He places an ear over the exact location of the pain, listens, holds out his wrist and checks his timepiece. He pulls away, looks at you, repeats the actions.

—Back in a minute, Billy, he says.

He returns with a small sack of what looks like a blue medicinal powder.

—What is it, you ask, a ground-up lizard or something? Some Jamaican cure-all? How much do I take?

—You don't take it, Captain. You burn it. And you repeat any magic words you know.

—Why call me Captain? You know how I feel about—

—Nothing more to call you, Captain.

So he knows.

—Mention it to the men, and I'll have you strapped into your cabin as a madman. For the good of the ship.

—I ain't worried. I got all the blue powder in Oceania. No one else got any.

While you ponder your condition, without sullenness or

rancor, you think of a diversion for your woman. She is angry because you neglected her in port, and she was beset by Gresham. Now you've stayed away one—make it two—days. She's in cabin three, lonely, wondering (as they always have) how she's let you down. She remembers suddenly that you have chided her gently about all those clothes she brought along.

So she tosses out a pair of slippers, finds that pleasant (her husband bought them), and throws out an expensive linen stole. This is visually, perhaps, the most photogenically intriguing idea you have come up with. Between the ports, linking the islands, leaving obvious clues as to your course, are expensive articles of women's clothing. They float on the sea, like huge blossoms. Changes in current, tidal shifts, the wake of passing vessels, cause them to move, expand and contract, assume different shapes. The sun bleaches and discolors them. And imagine the joy of a Polynesian woman when a garment catches on one of her mate's oars. The joy and then her simple, touchingly ephemeral disappointment when she discovers the dress will not fit.

You visited Barbara one day out of the first port and told her she was being foolish. In the next port, an ice-green peignoir fouled the propeller of the harbor pilot's motorboat. You fumed until she told you she was changing her life for you.

—Why?

—I want to be a sailor. I am your subordinate. I am in the lesser position and I should live accordingly.

You find that charming.

Suède jackets, dancing pumps, lounging robes, slacks, shorts, jumpers, a new lightweight mac, perfect for the tropical squall, gowns and gowns, feathered mules.

Floating ornaments, wavering over the great gouges in the

sea's floor, catching and pulling free on barrier reefs, washing up on the atolls. The ship moves; Barbara jettisons her identity; time passes.

You must indicate the passage of time through the use of a montage. Two themes are emphasized: movement and desire.

The first, movement, is depicted in the many ports of call; the loading and unloading of cargo; the young sailor's down which, at the end of the sequence, is a beard; the rust which is scraped away, reappears, is scraped again; studies of the ship's wake; hissing views of the prow cutting through clear water; sunrises following sunsets following sunrises; the trail of her clothing.

Desire is communicated through your entering and leaving cabin three. You go in, you come out. We see writhing on the bunk, feminine hands clutching your back. You go out. You come in. She bites your shoulder. You come out. She pours the brandy. You enter. She achieves climax with a shriek. You have a twinge. You go out. We see you bent over the charts. We see her massaging her flanks hysterically. You enter. We see her awakening at dawn, refreshed. You exit. She shouts your name: Bill, Bill!

The themes are tastefully mingled, never boring.

—Soon we will be going home. Do you think of your husband and daughters?

—Yes. With a little pity. But not much.

—Why pity?

—I pity people on land—every landlocked human being.

Her answer is so perfectly consistent with your attitudes, your philosophy, that you misinterpret that sudden heaving of your chest. You think it is joy and relief. But you are wrong. You are watching Barbara smile that cautious, hopeful way which begs your comment, your praise, and she recedes suddenly. You see her as if the lenses in the telescope have you reversed. She is small, too small, and flying back from you, still smiling.

I didn't regret anything until months after I got back. Then I found out he'd died. He had a bad heart. I always felt—well, pardon me, but, I felt as if I'd killed him.

That old woman did not kill you! You disregard what she says. You decide to change the resolution, ignore that selfish, dried-out, sagging bitch's explanation. Who knows if she is telling the truth?

You decide to die aboard the ship. You pick the perfect moment: the day Barbara has finally thrown away all her clothing. She calls Harvey and instructs him to go amongst the sailors—the smallest men—and purchase dungarees and chambray shirts, white cotton socks, a woolen watch cap.

Harvey tries, does his best, buys what he can. He also purchases a sewing kit. She begins to shorten the legs, to take in the waistbands. Meanwhile, you are in your cabin, charting a course home.

Why do you die? Not through such exertion as she would warrant or demand! No, it is something splendid. Is it a storm? Or does Harvey jump overboard, because he has used up the blue powder, burning it for you? (He never calls you Billy, now; never drops in for a chat.) What kills you?

It isn't important. You cannot think of the exact stress which finishes you off. Not that your mind is incapable of presenting you with the perfect dramatic excuse. You don't wish to bother; it isn't that important. What seem of far greater significance than the last little push, by nature, are the actions which follow your death. You almost hesitate to reveal them. You must.

You are dead. You are laid out in the tropics, in your bunk. Something about your lifelessness, so close upon vitality, so formal yet relaxed, reminds you of hawser, Flemished down. Why? No matter. Harvey has dressed you in the white dinner jacket. He has had to cut away part of the brim of your hat so that it will set upon your head at a respectable angle. It slides over your skull like a horseshoe, that cutaway rim.

All the crewmen and officers pass through your modest quarters. The austerity of the cabin amazes them.

—He no happy. No habee fun, Wong Lee comments.

—Bloke lived like a bloody monk, 'e did, says Charles Blackshire.

Gresham, for years waiting for this moment when he takes command, pauses at your side.

—Poor devil. Not yet fifty. But a real master. He taught me everything I know. The stuff you never get in a classroom. I hope I'll be half the man he was.

Barbara bursts in. She had not even finished sewing her trousers when the word came out over the intercom. She has to hold up her pants. She is brown and looks good, better than ever before, but she's out of her mind.

—Get out of here, all of you! Out out out! I have to be with him! I have questions! Out out out!

The men leave. Barbara kneels beside your bunk. She pleads with you to come back to life. She cannot live without you. She cannot go back home to her family. You made her a sailor. You gave her purpose and the sea. You can't be dead. Please. Please. She weeps.

It is the sort of maudlin, unscientific nonsense which you, as a living skipper, would never have tolerated.

Fortunately, Harvey is standing at the open hatch. He overhears her. He comes in.

—This isn't a big ship, missus, but we've got work for everyone. We'll give you a new job, me an' Fred.

—Fred?

—Captain Gresham. He's the new master.

Barbara rises, nods, walks out. She sees Gresham in the passageway. She intends to approach him, if need be to salute him, but she doesn't. For some reason he has chosen this occasion to wear another of his U-boat turtlenecks. It infuriates her. It is the symbol of a callowness. She will not stand for it.

—You're no captain! she says, contemptuously. Our captain is dead. There he lies.

Gresham tries to smile at the assembled men, tries to shrug off her insult, but she grabs at the neck of his sweater and pulls it. My God, it isn't even a sweater. It's a dickey! The men see this and turn their broad, solemn backs, the rigid backs of men deprived of leadership, on this grotesque revelation.

Then you arrange a burial at sea. The sailmaker sews a canvas shroud for you, stitches you in it. No one cares for such formality, but all the men know you must be wrapped in a cocoon, that the flag of some Scandinavian country will be draped over it, that a plank will be oiled, that weights will be attached to the shroud, and that Acting Captain Gresham will read a few words over you. Then you will be cut loose; you will slide down the plank, slip into the sea with scarcely a splash, sooner or later to be devoured by sharks. You've accepted this fate, though you hate to think you'll give strength and nourishment to sharks: that you will end as a tidbit for the enemies of sailors after having served the men for so long, for a lifetime.

So they assemble, all but Barbara, for the ceremony. The sailors attempt a hymn; the voices bark and scrape, hoot, crackle. They cannot remember the words. Gresham opens the book, scowling.

—We are gathered here today—

—Men of this ship, Barbara says. She is standing on the deck above, grasping the railing. She wears your winter hat and coat, brass buttons removed. The clothing hangs on her. The hat covers her eyes and most of her nose. Only her mouth is revealed with clarity.

—Men of this ship, if you bury your master now, you make that man there the true captain. If you wait until we return to port, he will be temporary, and we will feel the presence of the old master, the real master. Do you wish to serve a pipsqueak? Think of yourselves, forget duty and the dead captain. Your safety is at stake, your lives in balance.

—Don't risk your fates. Save that man. Use his presence as a wedge against this upstart swabbie, still wet behind the ears . . . and somewhere else, if you know what I mean.

Despite the solemnity, the men smile, begin nodding, whispering among themselves.

—You know your old skipper wanted a watery grave. But more than that, he wanted his ship to get through. For his sake, and for the sake of yourselves and your loved ones, don't dump him. Keep him aboard till we get home, to remind Gresham of what a real skipper means to his ship.

—Gob, the little lydie's got her point.

—Me no throw away Matter.

—Don't tilt the plank, Mr. Graverson.

That Gresham could not force through his obligations,

that he let this mutinous behavior disturb regulations, proves to you that he didn't learn his job under your command. Even though dead, you take note of this. It strikes you as sad commentary not only on Gresham but on the tribute Barbara pays you. You should have been dumped; that is the way of the sea.

And this is proved by the return voyage. Barbara never once cared about the ship or the men. She cared only about you. A matron, a mother, a beautiful, youthful, intelligent woman, and she has decided to prove to your corpse, now stowed and frozen in the meat locker, that *she* could be captain.

She ranges the decks, shouting orders. She screams at the helmsman to change his heading to 323°, shouts to the engine room, "Back full right rudder!" She peers for hours at the radarscope, sights whales, submarine periscopes. She orders the men to abandon ship at least once a day.

She moves into your bunk, occupies your cabin, studies your charts. Harvey has to steal the ship's log and give her the ship's inventory. She makes entries constantly.

June 17, 1600 hours: Larboard engine faltering.
Supplies gone. Fire rages in the forecastle.
We haven't much time left. The men keep looking
at me, waiting for my orders. I have none to
give. Oh, if we but had a true master!

Daily, with Harvey, she tours the ship, stopping at the meat refrigerator, where you are frozen to the vegetable crates which support you. She glances in at the chickens, the quartered beef on the meathooks, the crates of chops.

—Enough there to see us home, steward, she says. The owners will be pleased with that.

—Yes, sir, ma'm, Harvey says.

When the men disregard her orders as a captain, she acts like a woman. She tempts the crew. She appears in the forecastle, her face hidden, then laughs at the seamen who disobey her. If one so much as looks at her with the vaguest flicker of lust in his eye, she reports him to the acting captain.

Gresham's courtesy in the dining hall is laughed at. To his face she calls him "Mr. U-boat." To the other officers he is "that boy."

As they near port she tries everything to lead the ship astray. She steals into the radio shack and turns on all switches, announces incredible positions over the microphone, proclaims mayday—we've been rammed!—on the emergency frequency. She finds books on seamanship and steals into the flag locker at night, then begs and tries to bribe your electrician to hoist lights indicating that your ship is towing another vessel. Your crew, aware that Gresham is an incompetent and a weak-spined skipper, might be tempted by these offers. But, out of loyalty to you, they refuse.

And, of course, such loyalty pleases her. It keeps you alive for her. She repeats every idiotic idea she has many times. She glories in the plain sailor's halting, courteous refusal.

—Understand it ain't that I don't need the dough or don't hate this young feller enough to do him dirt, but I can't screw up with the real old man below down there in the freezer. Sorry, ma'am.

—Make me your skipper.

—Can't, ma'am. You ain't got the papers, beggin' your pardon, ma'am.

Slowly the ship continues.

On the day of the return home, she occupies the flying bridge from predawn hours. When the ship creeps through the crowded offing, awaiting emergency precedence due to your death, she begins howling the commands to the empty decks.

—Ease three! she screams. Take a strain on one! Hey, you bastards, slack off the bowline!

The men listen. They look up, hesitant and even ashamed, to see this beautiful woman raging at them in their own language, using words she cannot possibly understand.

—Double up! Secure it!

Yet they appreciate, those humble sailors, the animal dedication of this person. It reinforces their respect for you, lost now to the sea, soon to leave the ship forever.

—Damn me but he musta been a real devil with the women!

You know that nothing can separate the ship from its port, a man from his grave, a story from its ending. The ships come home or they are not ships but phantom craft. The railed cranes move out along the wharf tracks, the throw lines are readied aboard ship, the hatches are uncovered, the gangplank is lowered into place. You have arrived.

Barbara feels it. She sees her family gathered on the dock. Her husband smiles, waves one hand weakly. Her daughters gaze at their mother, their faces so young, so innocent, so expressive of confidence. Wife and mother, she stands now at the railing, her captain's hat over her ears, her captain's coat hanging to her knees. Just for a moment she realizes she is adorned for the sea and must change. But she recalls that she cannot change, having thrown away her shore finery.

—Mama. Here. Here! Mama, what are you wearing?

She will go ashore with your frozen corpse. If the ambulance driver will permit it, she will take a handle of the stretcher, will squat at the edge of the sweating shroud as it goes through the city, her eyes watching moisture bead and trickle on the canvas, and, without hope, she will pray. For herself, of course.

Then she will take you to the crematorium (Jeanne Moreau once more), and after you are ash, she will take the ashes. And perhaps, with ash secreted on her person, pressed against her flesh, forever, she will be able to return to the land and her family. Perhaps.

That woman who started the story did not, you are sure, wait for the ash. You are sure that she brought back cheap souvenirs and a frantic, unsteady gaze to her husband. As she did not mention children, you are not certain she had to trouble herself with them. But if there were children, you know that old woman warned them of the unsanitary conditions in the islands and told them nothing more.

You must forget her entirely. Refuse to remember her. Instead, reply again and again the film you have developed in your mind. It is at times sentimental; but it is comic in parts. And your death is a triumph.

Again and again replay your sea show. It is a tribute to you. Your masterpiece. Absolutely true.

GREASED SAMBA

Doc Bob: Questionnaire received and read through once. I'll answer, I think. Not likely to fool around with the "impressions" of Winifred Farms you ask for down near the bottom. I don't believe what you say. I think you sent this to find out why Sug passed away, had the bruises, smelled odd. That's what you're after, only you aren't man enough to come out straight and ask for it. I can't write small enough to get even "short answers" on your form sheet.

May never tell you, finish and not send. Or never finish.

My permanent address is here, with my daughter, and you already have the number. Three people in the house. Daughter, forty-two, her husband, about forty-five, and me. Granddaughter comes by all the time. She's pregnant, wants guidance, calls me Gram. But I'm with just the two, Will and Sue, and I have a room to myself and run of the house.

Health fine. Bruises—I had plenty—are all gone. Smell— I smelled too—remains, I think, because my daughter is sniffing around. You must have spilled all the beans you could, Doc Bob, but you couldn't explain anything. Hips hurt sometimes, pains in the lower back region, but they were hurting worse at Winifred Farms and I got by. Eyes water. Television makes them water. Not the shows, the light. Tired sometimes more than others. Health good.

"Mental attitude" sharp. Can remember whatever is necessary when it's necessary. Can cut out the rest if I want. Sharp, but sometimes down. Sug, of course, bothers me. Had to happen. We knew it would, both of us. Forty-six years, three months, seven days (a week). Don't have to think of that, though. I can stop it, any time, say no to myself and the wheels lock. My secret of success right there. Think what you want to think.

Trying to keep the answers short. Suppose you want brief answers so we won't wear out. So you won't be responsible.

Next question is stupid: We came to Winifred Farms because we had to. Just like you used to say, after the "hard part" you deserve a long vacation. I can see you clearly, sitting at your desk, in your shorts and sandals, your head shining, telling us about the "long vacation," when we first became interested.

I had the money for it. I could afford Winifred Farms. I could have afforded better places. I own three shoe stores, in the Bellflower–Norwalk area, and it's an inexpensive line, competing with Karl and Gallenkamp, and I'm doing fine. My son-in-law, Will, is. He took over.

I liked the looks of the place. The strung-out cottages, and the orchards. I liked your helper, Hemley, and old Dick Watson, who was Volunteer Host to Sug and I. It was quiet. We could have gone to France or Egypt. Sug, when she found out about our great-grandchild, wanted to be around for the birth.

Cottages. Cottage seventeen was fine. I want to be exact, whether it takes a long answer or not. I didn't like the padding in the shower. I didn't like, at first, the handrailing in the hallway.

That railing is a little loose now, by the way. The new occupants ought to be told that.

I didn't like the exposure much. If you get up early, you like the light to come right into the house. There, I had to go outside. I used to watch it start some mornings under the trees. Sug slept late. I sat out on the porch, watched it. First thing I knew the trunks lit up. You'd see one, then four, then a dozen thin trunks, and then you could make out the leaves at the top, the shape of the tree at the top. All right there, day after day. But it was too cold in the winter. The cottages ought to have been built facing the other way. For the exposure.

General comments on recreation and entertainment. Hell, if you remember me and Sug—Sugar and Hank, they called us, in case you have forgotten—you know we loved the games. We won every prize we ever tried for: the three-legged Jello-in-a-spoon race, and the two-couple egg-in-a-spoon relay, with Ike and Mary Fellers. Ike and I won all the men's three-legged races. Somewhere I've got a dozen Polaroid snapshots of Sug and I and the others that they put in the crepe-paper wreath on the bulletin board. The Victors. Smiling, holding up our cups of victory punch.

II

I got a little tired there yesterday, so I quit and went to find the pictures. Found them.

All evening I thought about this form. Just like you to send something like this months after. Lot I'd forgot. It's coming back—probably too much for the short answers.

Going back to recreation and entertainment. I enjoyed the rock hunts. First entertainment at Winifred Farms. Liked it three times, three Hunts, then I didn't like it. "Rock Hunt Today. Don't forget rock hats and rock bags!" I asked Hemley about the bulletin. He said: "Hank, it's just that a bunch of us go up into the hills behind Santa Ana and look at rocks." I asked if he thought Sug and I would enjoy that. He said: "Might find it interesting, Hank. Might not. Gets you out in the air." No selling, just straight answers from Hemley. You got yourself a good helper.

I guess this is an impression, out of place on the form, but what I thought of last night when I was resting was standing out on the side of the hill when it was getting dusk in the valley. I thought of the wind blowing, curling the brims of our straw hats, and tugging at the women's skirts, and blowing away the voices.

Scattered—Hemley turned us loose—those that could walk all right, and we'd stand about ten yards apart. Stoop over, fill the bags with rocks, then pull them out one by one, dropping them. I never knew there was such a variety of rocks. Weights all different, sizes different. And the colors, the veins of color, the patterns.

You'd hear Mary Fellers call: "Ike, looky here. A green one."

The wind ripped up the words. They came out: "I look ear. Green."

Like that. From all over. The voices, croaking, and all the words torn.

"Found one think gold."

"Green cat eye."

"Hank quartz."

Hatbrims shuddering, rough edges curving down almost into our eyes, and the wind sharp enough to make your eyes water, and the women's skirts blowing. The hems flapping. Shadows short against the scrub brush and the stones. There was always sun, but down in the valley, along the floor of the valley, it was dusk. It got gray. Night coming up out of the ground. Like smoke coming up.

"Found think gold."

"Green eye."

"Hank."

Voices chopped right off as the words came out.

Pick up a rock, warm in your hand, hold it and weigh it and squint to see the colors, the grain, the shape. Drop it. Take another rock.

III

I stopped. Tired. Granddaughter came by. Puffing. Stands with her legs apart, belly so heavy it pulls her spine forward. Wears a cheap flat heel without any arch support.

Not as pretty as her mother. Who's not as pretty as *her*

mother was. Well, you wouldn't know, never saw Sug when she looked like she did.

Well, the rock hunts at the beginning, until I got to finding the same rocks, on the third trip, and the racing, and the Along Nature's Trails trips, and the picnic. Even the Annual Winifred Farms Luau. The one we went to. The idea seemed fine.

I never like a game where you have to sit down to participate. Never went to a book discussion. Never talked politics, because I know what's right. Croquet? As Dick Watson used to say: "Croquet, OK." For most of my life you couldn't catch me on a dance floor.

That's true too. Maybe ten times I danced with Sug while we were married, in forty-six years. And then, just at the end, we were dancing fools.

If you're surprised, you should be. That's the secret. I may tell it.

Shuffleboard—old Dick Watson ruined that for me.

You and Hemley never knew about that game that Dick played and how he cared about it, or you would have had more sense than to treat him the way you did. Now that's how I feel. I knew him. I used to sneak a cigar with him now and then. You didn't know him, if you want my opinion. Blood pressure's one thing, just one thing. You can ask a man to piss in a bottle, or do any other damned awful business you want, to get to know something about him, but you won't know it all.

I figure when you read this you'll start scratching your knees and smiling. And a little more sweat will spring out on your skull, coming out of the pores, where the hair should be. Not that it's any fault of yours. Men get bald. Although, you'll admit, yours is a very special case. You always reminded us of someone else who is bald—someone famous.

The reason that Dick Watson got so mad at the shuffleboard game that day was that he was the best player, by a long shot, of all those amateurs at Winifred Farms. Only Bill Dawson and Ike ever beat him, and they might win a game out of every five. Old Dick showed everybody how. That particular morning he lost three games in a row. He was nervous, he said later, because it was a tournament and he wanted his name right back up there, on the top of the list. He liked having his name there.

That's why he called the court a sonofabitch. And broke his stick.

Then you came in from your damned gardening, with your shorts on and khaki shirt with the sleeves cut off. And them damned sandals. Your toes dirty, looking like potatoes just dug up. And you start making up to everyone but going after Dick.

"Before you play again, Dick, I think you ought to weigh those markers and watch the courts getting waxed. Supervise the waxing."

I remember the way you turned around and winked at everybody. You wrinkled your forehead, raising eyebrows you don't have.

I'll tell you what I think, Doc Bob. I think your advice killed Dick Watson. He never played shuffleboard again,

never went to the recreation hall again, because he couldn't
weigh the markers, couldn't go and watch the waxing. Hell,
you knew he wouldn't. From then on he watched television
and came over to my place for a cigar in the evenings.
Clara Watson had a broken hip, you remember. Do you
remember us at all? And she was a little silly, anyway. Had
every reason to be and was.

Yes, we smoked cigars.

He quit the rock hunts when I did. He couldn't get in on
the sports because of his feet. He never liked the Along
Nature's Trails trips. The longer bus rides bothered his
kidneys. You must have records.

It was you that insisted we keep "occupied." He couldn't
bring himself to weighing the markers. He quit. And it
wasn't too long afterward that he passed on.

I want to stop here and say something for the last time.
When I got stuck in the bus toilet, that had nothing to do
with Dick. And the reason I didn't yell was that I didn't
want to scare Sug. When Hemley noticed I was gone for a
long time, he came and tapped at the door, and I answered
him calmly. I don't know why I should have yelled. You
should have those doors made so you can unlock them from
the outside. And not have to take them off if someone
gets stuck. We were on our way to San Juan Capistrano,
and they had to stop the bus and unhinge the door to get
me out. This upset Sug and everybody.

I didn't like being stuck in there. But I didn't get stuck
because of Dick Watson and I couldn't pull the bolt back
and I saw no reason to scream. That's it. And down here
where you say "evaluation of staff," I'd say you ought to go

on back to medical school and find out that it is wrong to hint to a woman of advanced years that her husband is grieving the loss of a friend so much he's shutting himself up in bus toilets.

Your hints started us going to the dances and that is the reason she died, in part, because we thought—you thought —we'd better be more social.

I won't say I'm holding you responsible.

I'm quitting now. I get angry thinking about this. I'm not tired. I shouldn't get so angry. I'm sweating. Like your bald head.

IV

Missed two days. Worn out yesterday. Slept, read a little, decided not to finish this. Then I couldn't sleep last night. Kept seeing you at your desk, reading this, eating home-grown fruit. You're well set up now but you'll get fat sooner or later. That fruit, you can't eat even that all the time, without getting fat. Keeps you regular you said. Didn't keep you regular as far as your hair's concerned, did it?

You got my feelings about the "community and social organizations" except for the square dancing.

I didn't like that. I hate that slippery stepping, and the music, and the callers. Only tried it once.

But what I may as well tell you about organization that I forgot to mention above is the way you handle the passing on of people at Winifred Farms. It is a disgrace and I despised it. That is, when I found out old Dick Watson had passed on that night, I found it out the next morning when I was going out to participate in some kind of a leaf study and there was the sign on the bulletin board saying he was dead. And the memorial services were to commence almost immediately.

I had a sports shirt on and a pair of blue yachting sneakers —deck wear, we call it—and I had to go in right then and pray, standing on the shuffleboard court. Old Dick's mortal remains were already on the way to Pomona. Clara gone too.

I'm sure you're right. Memorial services are bad enough, when you get caught in one where you hardly knew the party, and the sooner they're done the better. But Dick and I were close. He hated cigars, called them "stinkers," and came over to seventeen for one almost every evening. Half the time he couldn't take more than about a quarter before he had to throw it out. He kept coming.

Teal-blue deck wear. I see the idea. But there was Willis Townsend, who Dick hated, praying for his "safe passage." And all of it over then. Amen, and it's done.

Sug missed it. I went back, told her Dick was dead, told her I'd been to the services, and heard that Clara had been sent off. She couldn't believe it. She asked me to repeat all. I did. She asked if I thought Clara had known that Dick was sick, if she'd spent his last hours at his side. I said I didn't know. I still don't.

But you get it all done so fast—and I can see why—that it scared Sug. What if one of us got sick suddenly? Would the other know? Scared me too.

V

Today I'll tell you about the square dances, and the other dances, and let's see if you can keep smiling and raise what should be eyebrows and wink.

They've got a name for you at Winifred Farms. I won't tell it.

I'll tell you something else that'll open your eyes. Make you put aside your apple for a minute.

We went to one lesson and got in with that slick-stepping crowd that look like the senior citizens you see on television. You see the lights shining on their eyeglass frames and their grins. They keep their teeth clenched and keep grinning, everyone panting like heat-struck dogs, so when you're close you hear wind whistling through dentures. And spit crackling and spattering on their stretched lips. They get this kind of skating step, specially the men, and they paw at the ground, and come scooting down the middle while everybody claps and grins and winks at each other in the next formation.

I'll admit we made fools of ourselves that first night, when they were trying that reel and that bunch tried to show us how to do-si-do, where you come down between the two ranks of people. I saw one man come down backward and cross in front of his partner and skip up to the end of the line, and he never looked over his shoulder. And I was just mad enough to try it without looking. All right, not looking because I didn't want to be outdone.

And I did hear Sug call out: "Hank," when we were three-quarters of the way down. So I looked back, but when I moved to the right, she moved to her left.

Bang. We crashed.

Fell right over on our hands and knees. Both of us lost our glasses (but they didn't break, either pair). And I looked around at her, and she looked around at me.

Everybody else was whooping around, trying to get us up, but we, Sug and I, just stayed there, on our hands and knees, and looked at each other, after we found our glasses, and then, by God, we started laughing. Weren't hurt, not a bit, and not a bit scared, and not ashamed, even though everybody began to bray, when they discovered we were all right.

I said back there I was mad. All right, I was mad because of the can in the bus and the way you got rid of Dick when I had on a Hawaiian shirt and canvas wear. And the skatey-footed step the experts used.

I was mad! Hell yes. So we went to the dancing lesson and fell down—I knocked my wife down. But something happened. It didn't hurt. Hitting each other didn't hurt.

You couldn't understand that. You saw us winning the three-legged races, keeping the Jello in the spoon, our two old inside knees tied together with a scarf. And how we counted to ourselves, paced ourselves, and pulled ahead of Willis and Lily and the others. You saw us when Will and Sue came over, or my granddaughter, and the women would come up the walk carrying packages, sometimes balancing them on the unborn baby, and they wouldn't even let me take a sack. You saw what you thought was mooning over

Dick's passing on. Or getting into the bus before the pig was served at the luau, because we said we were tired. We were tired. Only you don't have even a suspicion of why we were tired.

You're better off with a specimen, baldy.

Two days after we hit and fell, in the afternoon, while "The Jolson Story" was playing, I heard a funny noise from the kitchen. It was a quiet part in the movie; I think Al was telling his old dancing partner he wanted him to be his manager. I was watching, Sug was supposed to be washing dishes. I heard her slippers tapping on the linoleum. I walked in there. Here she came, back to me, skipping down the length of the kitchen between the sink and the stove. I started clapping.

"You try," she said.

"No room," I said.

Carpet in the living room. Bedroom too small. Hallway then. That's where we tried.

We danced in the hall that first time, tried it about three times, and got tired. We went in to sit down, take a breather. I said I figured with a few more practice sessions we'd be as good as any of them slick-footed dancers. She said she agreed, she guessed. Then I said I didn't care much if we never went back, because that first fall, just when my glasses were gone, and I thought I'd hurt her, hitting her so hard, and then all of the grinners came around and tried to haul us up, that fall had bothered me, and I figured when we laughed and got them to laughing we had sort of made ourselves out to be the comedians.

She stopped me: "You didn't hurt me, Hank."

Well, I said I was afraid I had. And then she said she was afraid she'd hurt me, because she was a little heavy, and moving fast. I said I didn't think she was heavy, and that it was my old bones that were dangerous.

"They never were dangerous, Hank," she said.

I won't tell you what she looked like. I won't tell you what that reminded me of, the way she looked, then, looking right in my eye saying my old bones had never hurt her.

You wouldn't know. You never were like I was. I don't know if you ever had a hair on your head. Would you have any idea what it would be, in the middle of the afternoon, with Al singing "Rosie, You Are My Posie," a song I first heard when I was a grown man, not a kid, and to be dancing?

What we did, then, was get up and try one more dance down the hallway. It was late enough so you couldn't see well. The halls are poorly lighted, anyway, because of the poor exposure. One more dance, backward, starting with the clickety-clickety click. Down we came. Hearing the slippers tap and slide, getting louder, heard each other breathing, louder, tried to guide by the dark wall, the rail, but couldn't.

Wham!

Both of us slid forward. We didn't fall. We caught the rail! That safety rail in cottage seventeen. It's weak.

Because we caught ourselves when we started to fall. And with the other hand, held onto our glasses. But the next time we put our glasses down.

The next time was only a minute later when we decided to try again without hitting but hit again anyway.

Wham!

There. That's why the bruises. A couple more times. That was it. The smell was a kind of ointment I bought and had delivered from a druggist. It was a grease. I put it on the rail.

One night we danced too late and I got so tired I fell asleep. It was after the *luau*. She passed on while I was sleeping.

That's all. That's why I left. That's why she passed on. I haven't got any other comments. No, I wouldn't think of returning.

VI

I don't know why I'm afraid to tell the truth. Sug wouldn't be. I'll tell you why and you'll spit out apple seeds into your palm, and put them in the empty ashtray, and rub your hairless knees and think, and smile, raising what should have been eyebrows and batting what should be eyelashes, and then you'll nod and think you got it all. Figure it out. Piss in a bottle. Only you'll be wrong.

We danced every day for about a week, until we could hardly walk. We hit. On purpose? We turned the lights out when it was day or waited until night, and neither one of us said anything at all—couldn't—only one or the other would get over there, at one end of the hall, facing the other way, and start tapping heels and then he'd hear the other set of heels start clicking and wait, until finally one or the other set of heels went *click*. Then down we'd go. *Wham!*

Right back, start again. *Click*. And the clicking and breathing getting louder, then: *Wham!*

Until one or the other couldn't hold on to the rail or just had to leave, walk out of the room, go in somewhere, sit down, hips and hind ends (at least mine) aching. Some mornings I didn't get out of bed. Couldn't. Or she couldn't. Whoever could brought the food.

A week. And one day, when it was me in bed, and she just barely out, she said: "How bad are you hurt?" It was the first time we said anything, I guess. Because we couldn't talk about it. I won't say why. I can't.

I had some pretty big old bruises. In fact my backside was covered. Hers was too, she said. And one hip was in bad shape.

She'd brought in a tray with prune juice and toast and Sanka. She had on a robe. Her hair was still mussed up. She wasn't wearing glasses. She looked pretty worn out. She said she didn't want to go see Doc Bob—you—about the hip because then he'd see the bruises. So, she said, she reckoned we'd better quit. For a while, she said. Until we saw if the hip healed. No more dancing.

We didn't talk about it because we were ashamed. If that's what you're thinking. But if you got sense enough just try to imagine what two senior citizens like myself and Sug would say, if we decided to talk, about what we were doing. And remember we didn't hate it.

Remember she said until we saw if the hip healed or not.

It never healed. Hurt her that last month like nothing you could dream of, Mr. Clean. That's who you remind me of, only he has eyelashes and brows. Mr. Clean. Both of us used to call you Mr. Clean. In fact, a hell of a lot of the people call you that. *A lot.* Ike and Mary do. Dawson. They whisper it: "Here comes Mr. Clean." What are you going to do about it? Kick them out? They pay your way. You can't.

Waiting, Mr. Clean, until the hip healed, but it didn't heal. And we began to get worried, thinking she'd have to go see you. I suggested she go out, to another doctor, and have an X ray made. We were going to, in fact, right after the Annual Winifred Farms Luau.

VII

Mr. Clean, I almost quit but didn't.

I suppose you're thinking the hula dancer did it. No. It was getting in the bus, and having so much trouble lowering ourselves in the seat, and then my having to go to the can again, while we were traveling, and her saying: "Careful." And then looking sorry after she said it.

And then, when we were down at the beach, and the pig wasn't quite done, and all the others were waiting around there at the tables with their paper plates and silverware in their hands, and some of them with napkins tucked down in their shirts, and the lot repeating: "Boy, there's a pig I'll eat." "There's a *pig* for you." "I could eat her all." On and on. Laughing, nervous, hungry, sniffing the smoke off the meat. Sug said we ought to take a walk down the beach. We did, and it was hard getting up out of those picnic tables, out from behind the stationary benches, hard walking down that sandy incline. We crossed to the wet sand, but by the time we got there, her shoes were full.

I said I'd empty them. I started to stoop down. I knew right away I'd have trouble. My whole lower back region ached. And from the picnic tables you could hear everybody laughing. I suppose someone else, probably Willis Townsend, had just said that he could eat the whole pig by himself. I looked up, toward the rise, where they were.

"I could walk down a ways," Sug said. "Because you'll have to take the shoe off. I can't."

So we walked down, out of earshot, out of view. I fell down on my knees. Just dropped. And she put one hand on my head for the balance, and lifted each foot.

She put a lot of weight on me. A couple of times she almost fell, but she caught herself. It pained her to stand on one foot. And I had trouble getting the laces undone, because of the light off the sand—made my eyes water. And there was sand in her anklets. I had to take them off. She wore a wool athletic sock.

It was the first time I'd seen her feet in years. They felt cold when I brushed them off.

She had to help me up, pull on me, and she had terrible pains.

So we went back to the bus, got right in the bus, sat down together, and someone—one of the Hawaiian boys—brought us our paper plates. We never saw the hula-hula dancing at all. We sat and talked. We didn't talk about dancing at all. We talked about the great-grandchild, and whether Sue and Will ought to buy a house, the one I'm living in, and what the food tasted like. We didn't mention anything about the sand, or dancing. But I knew, when we pulled away that evening, when it was all over, and everybody got on the bus with them *leis* around their necks, and all of them fell asleep with their chins half-buried in flowers, I knew that we'd dance that night.

We did. Not right away. We turned on the television when we got home, and both of us were dog-tired. There was one of those Mexican programs on from over in East L.A. And someone was demonstrating the samba, a dance where the dancers don't touch, but just kind of rock back and forth, and move their arms slowly, and sometimes pass behind one another. Maybe you know it. I doubt that.

Sug said: "There's a dance. We could try that." And she tried. It was just rocking, you bend your shoulders forward, and you bend them back, and you move your arms. By the time she got started, the demonstration was over, the music finished.

I said: "That's a hip dance too, Sug. That'll hurt."

"Hurting right now," she said, and kept on rocking. "You don't have to bend so much."

So I tried. Without music it was easier, because you could set your own pace. We rocked back and forth, and got damned tired.

She started to pass by me, rocking in and out, slowly, like that. And we just sort of touched. Hip bones. I've thought this over so many times. When we just brushed she groaned, just a little, whimpered.

My idea about the grease. Get the grease, cover our clothes with it, then we'd slide. I wanted to dance. She wouldn't stop. We rubbed the grease over the outside of our clothes

standing side by side at the kitchen table. Then we started
again. Just one slight brush. "Oh!" she whispered.
Then another, light. I grunted.

Want to quit?

No.

Ungh.

They got harder. Before long they were just as hard as ever.
Before long we quit moving our arms. We quit swaying. We
just circled each other, stepping back when we were facing,
and with our glasses off, so we couldn't see, and then
coming in, hard.

Wham.

Wham!

VIII

I had to quit. Now, I'll go quickly. Sometime along the way
I fell down and slept on the floor, and I guess she just kept
circling until whatever it was, a vein, broke open in her
brain and killed her. Killed her.

The grease was cold cream and Crisco, a combination, since
we didn't have much of either. That's the source of the
smell.

Now you understand. And I'm tired.

What we did, and we—Sug and I—killed her, I don't mind.
She didn't either. I'm going to send this to you. I don't care.

I suppose you think that's funny when a senior citizen whose
wife is dead—who helped kill his wife—says he doesn't care.

Doesn't care if he woke up one morning on the sofa in cottage seventeen and found his Sug dead in the living room, on the floor, smeared with Crisco and cold cream, bruised.

Go out and pick yourself an apricot, Doc Bob, and sit back under a tree and get your hairless head to working. Figure it out why we danced the greased samba. You'll never know. Mr. Clean. And I don't care if I do ruin their little joke. They'll find another one.

You'll never know any more than I've told you and you won't get any more out of me.

That's it. And no, I don't want to return to Winifred Farms, and won't. Never.

AN OFFERING

September 27

Dearest Cindy:

I am so sorry. So horrified. I can say nothing that doesn't sound empty and stupid.

I do hope you received the cable before you heard about the aircraft on the television or read of the accident in the newspapers.

This morning debris was found which they were able to identify positively.

I put him on the plane. I say this to help you, for I fear you might entertain useless hopes. No one knows why it crashed. The weather was perfect. God, I can't go on.

People here send their condolences.

Please, please, write!

Love,
Don

September 29

Dearest Cindy:

Still no word from you. I wrote my mother and asked her to call you, in case she hasn't done so on her own.

What has bothered me most is the idea that you might have been gone somewhere when it happened. But of course you would have met him at the airport. You know. Here is the text of the cable I sent the evening of the 25th.

Flight 249 lost over gulf. Sean aboard.
Please contact friends. Stay with same.
Write. Letter follows.

It was about midway across when radio contact was lost (you undoubtedly know this). No one has any idea what happened. The weather was perfect.

I cannot express how I feel. I know I insisted that you send him here this summer. Perhaps my letters were harsh. But I intended only to impress upon you the fact that he is still my son, despite what has happened between us. Although I have a family here, I could not simply ignore him—or our years together.

But I hope you understand that I cannot apologize for his death without accepting responsibility for it. And if I felt responsible I would kill myself.

Cindy, I found I could love unselfishly this summer. Sean was a difficult boy. He was tense, demanding, often brazenly independent. He had all the makings of the man I would like to have been. He had characteristics of yours too. He brought back to me a lot of what was so pleasant for so long between us.

I hope you will remember our pleasant times. Don't do anything foolish. Contact your new friends, stay with them.

Call my mother. She often asks about you and has been very sad because you refused to let her see her grandson.

Berta, and all your other friends here, send you their sympathies. Even little Aurelia (our daughter) loved her stepbrother.

Write. Tell me you are well and safe. And that you are facing this with the calmness that I would expect from the mother of such a fine boy.

Love,
D

October 4

Dear Cindy:

Your strange letter came today. Mistakenly, Berta read it. She is quite upset. I tried to explain to her that you are distraught and cannot be held responsible for all your thoughts, not at a time like this. I tried to convince her that the letter was in no way an indication of your ability to reason.

For me, however, the letter was a sad echo of those hysterical moments when we were breaking up. Even Berta's furor—which was temporary—seemed to repeat our agony of a few years back, when you began the mysterious telephone calls. But I don't think it is necessary to speak of that.

Cindy, it is preposterous—surely you know it is—to think that I would put a "device" in his luggage.

Of course I "hate to grow old." You must remember my fondness for the poem "To His Coy Mistress," by Andrew Marvell. I quoted it often enough to you. It is the only poem I remember from all those years of college, of jumping from major to major, never satisfied. You could, obviously, say that my remaining a student for so long, and marrying a younger woman the second time, was in fact an attempt to beat back the sound of "Time's wingèd chariot."

But Sean was not "evidence" of my age. Surely you must realize that he was a tribute—bright, moody, complex. I live in a culture not my own, and I have a daughter who will mature in this culture, which shapes its women in a way that is not my own. Even Berta has grown up in this tradition of Mariolatry (the worship of the Virgin Mary); she too manifests its tiresome effects, on occasion. The baby having been born, the conception having been "maculate," she is inclined to let go, physically and emotionally, unless reminded to do otherwise.

But that is not your concern. Your concern is to keep your intelligence and strive for self-control. Our son died in a terrible aircraft accident. *Neither* of us is guilty of any crime or complicity, unless loving the boy without thought of effects is a crime against oneself. That may be. Surely we should not punish ourselves for loving him unselfishly and totally.

Cynthia, I now train people to operate a computer which, when fed too much inaccurate or disorderly information, actually destroys itself. The technical explanation for this phenomenon is beyond your scope, but what happens is that the machine itself breaks down, mentally, if you will, and must be repaired extensively before it can function again.

You are not a machine. But you are infinitely more sensitive and delicate. Do not permit the knowledge that Sean is gone to destroy you. Get help if you feel you need it, or if you feel you are in any danger.

Sincerely,
Donald

October 5

Cindy:

Just after mailing a letter to you yesterday I received one from my mother. In it she explained why you think I have not cut off child support.

Surely you know better than that!

Don

October 10

Cynthia:

Two insurance investigators arrived at my home this morning at about ten. Berta, who has been distraught by recent events, was shocked to find that these men had heard Sean was being kept captive in my house.

You had better get some help and quickly. (I seem to have been giving you that advice for years.)

You are hurting Berta with your antics. I am perfectly willing to suffer the effects of your hysteria (I was once used to it), but I will not permit her to be punished. Heretofore I have not mentioned finances and have not stopped sending child support. I did not do so because I am sure you are in no mood to worry about money.

Now I feel I must begin to reconsider our arrangements. Perhaps if you were less dependent you would be forced to behave in a more realistic manner.

D.

P.S. I am coming to New York at the end of the year for a meeting. If you persist in this harassment, I will engage a lawyer while there to protect my family from your wild accusations.

October 18

Cynthia, my friend without knowing it, your son is not here in my house with us. Only is little Aurelia here, sleeping near me now when I write the illiterate letter in your language.

Merciful Christ, you are saying things that are so untrue! We have no one but our baby. Your Sean was here, yes, but he is gone forever! I am sorry for it! VERY!

My husband's superior, a very fine friend, engineering chief of the government here (your government) comes to our house with a photograph of your letter sent to a office. How could you write this?

I love the spirit in your Sean, but he pulled the bottle from Aurelia and sometimes climbed beneath her bed to make noise and shake the leg. I would not want to disturb my baby, with her quiet, beautiful face and holy fingers on the cloth now.

He brought to my husband question. What kind of man he is? We had to fight, my Donaldo and I. Never before!

I don't do anything to spite you in all of this.

With friendliness,
Berta

December 6

Cynthia. The packages and the letter arrived today. Quit it now! Don't spend your money on presents. Of course, the locket is beautiful.

As to the letter, I cannot imagine your having written it. Of course the season depresses you. But you are confusing your symbols and purposes. Sean was a solid, healthy, inquisitive boy. I see no equation. Your grief is enormous and has none of the elements you attribute to the Virgin Mary. (I mention her in a totally different context! Reread the letter of October 4.)

I will continue sending you child support until the approximate amount of your gifts to my family has been compensated for.

Please do not continue to write about religious matters. As you know, Berta had to marry me in a civil ceremony and she has been very upset of late about Aurelia's position concerning the church.

You do seem slightly more hopeful. I hope that is so.

D.

December 14

Cruel and crazy woman without dignity! Bruja! Your second filth came today! My husband will not do *this* and be my husband. How sinful you are! Where is your pride?

He must go to New York for business. I cannot take Aurelia into that northern cold. But he will not venture to see you in the West. He knows this!

He loves his small wife and beautiful child!

He does not think he is a "god." How can you treat this holy life so frivolous? You are the Virgin? NEVER!!!!!

Never write again your infamous documents of evil.

Berta

I send back all your gifts.

December 14

Dear Cynthia:

I received your second letter at home. Berta got it first, opened and read it, and out of hatred for you, she would not speak to me. She would have torn it up. I had to fight to get it from her.

You are too harsh on her. Remember, she is young and a child of a different culture. She *is* religious, so I'm afraid your flattering application of religious parallels to the human condition were far from pleasant to her. She did not find them at all consoling. She found it sinful, your calling Sean "your" Christ. She laughed (she won't agree that I am not responsible for the letter) at your notion that I am "your" God.

I did not laugh—though I could scarcely take the parallel, concerning me, seriously—because I understand that you want a child, that you need one, sincerely and totally, if you are to be whole.

As to your proposal, you must see that it is fantastic. Am I wrong in assuming that you too are beginning to hear "time's wingèd chariot," that your life has somehow summited; that time and energy wane; and that you feel the long downhill run commenced? As I have always felt, since I was a young man?

Perhaps for you too the attraction to frenzied ill-considered actions, such as your "proposition," becomes more compelling, somewhat as our divorce and my second marriage were to me years ago. Not, of course, that I did not love, or do not love, Berta.

I won't see you when I'm in the country. But I must say I find your last letter, which finally explains the actions of these months following Sean's death, as a good sign, a signal that, underlying your precipitateness, there was that sort of fervor of imagination, born of the sense of one's own in-effectuality, which makes complete sense to me.

Perhaps, while in New York, I will call you. A chat might be good for us both. We haven't talked in years.

Please take care of yourself.

Affectionately,
D.

P.S. I have written this at work. I don't want to disturb Berta with it. Please don't refer to the contents in future letters.

December 21

Donaldo: Where are you? I have called your hotel in the day and in the night.

Where? I will call the police, the airline!

If you ventured to Los Angeles you have *no home here!* No family! NO CHILD!

With the approach of the nativity, remember your obliga-tion.

Are you a pig? Answer at once.

Am I your loving wife?
Berta

NITELIFE

Don't worry when you go into Fuller's Nitelife for the first
time. It's an ordinary bar—dim, with a dusty juke, a pool
table, a small area for dancing. Nothing unusual, and the
regular customers are about as nice a bunch as you'll meet
anywhere. Only once in a while some nut off the street,
who has just lost his job or his wife, or who is remembering
what it was like in the marines, will come in spoiling. Then
you have to go easy, for your own sake. There's no bouncer,
and Stuffy can't do anything. (His stomach's no bigger than
a walnut after the last ulcer operation; he always says he has
to eat marshmallows in quarters, and soak them first; he always says it's a good thing he quit boozing, because with a
stomach like that he couldn't empty a jigger in an hour.
Stuffy hasn't had a drink since '52.)

Anyway, on your first time in, you run this risk: you can
be sitting there, drinking a beer right after work, maybe looking at yourself in the mirror, thinking you don't look bad,
bring on the women, when this tough comes up, for no

reason, and starts bad-mouthing you. He says you're ugly, or he asks what makes you think you're somebody, or he just bumps you, for no reason. Certainly, you don't provoke him. You're quiet. It's a peaceful hour. You can't understand what's going on. You look up, hardly have time to focus your eyes on this tiger's face.

Chop.

You're on your tail, your barstool's fallen over you, and your mouth feels like it's full of railroad ties. You feel the grit of tooth chips on your tongue.

". . . outa here now or I'm callin' the cops!" You hear Stuffy, mad as hell, shouting.

"Poor man," a woman says, and she gives you a hand getting up.

Blood. The lip is throbbing. "I didn't do nothing," you say. "I was just sitting there, for the love of Christ. What kind of place is this?"

"Go on back and wash off, and I'll buy you a drink," Stuffy says. "It's a good place."

In the can you see it isn't all that bad. You got a fat lip. You can feel the broken skin with your tongue, and the sharp edge of a tooth. You wash up, comb your hair. Before you're done the blood stops.

Not so bad. Wasn't there a woman there helped you?

Love at the Nitelife

Right away you get a feeling about Carol. She's not beautiful, but she has a lot of dignity in her face. It's a face that has seen a lot and yet it hasn't changed. It isn't bitter. It is maybe a little cautious.

She's thin, tallish, a little stooped from all those years as a waitress. She's got powerful arms. She doesn't spend all her money on crazy clothes, either. And you like that hairstyle; it reminds you of someone, sometime, when you were younger, maybe when you still lived at home. God, you can't remember when or who. You must be getting old.

"I had a father. He didn't give a damn for me or my brother. And my mother died, early, when I was six or so. The old man beat us. He was a real drunk. When he had money he never bought us food or clothes. We lived like pigs. When I was fifteen, I kissed my brother good-bye. I got out on the highway early one morning. I figured whatever happens can't be worse than this. I just said so long Texas and stuck out my thumb.

"The first guy, Ben, was good, a good man, but married. But he did everything he could for me. I mean any money he had left over from supporting his family he gave me. I had to work, waiting tables, and it made him mad he couldn't support me, 'cause he loved me, he really did. But he lost his job and had to move just when I was pregnant.

"Jesus, Joe, I had to give that baby away." Her upper lip is quaking. "I wanted it; I couldn't keep it; I had to give it away; I only know it was a boy and he got a good home, a good family.

"That's the worst thing I ever did in my life, giving that kid away; it's the worst, I'll never forgive myself. Never."

She cries.

You offer comfort. You tell her she was just a kid, poor and scared, not even married. What else *could* she do? "Anyway, face it, Carrie, the kid's probably got a nice life."

She agrees. Sure. Sure. But how would you like to have that hanging over your head all your life?

You tell her about your ex-wife, who wouldn't have kids, no matter what. She was afraid she would spoil her figure. You tell her what it's like to be driving truck night and day, and come home after a three-state run, and find she's run up a huge dentist bill.

"This is the kind of person she was," you say. "She had perfect teeth, you know, only they were just a little uneven in color, you know. So she gets 'em capped. Cost hundreds. God, she was vain. She sunk all my money in clothes. She had to have a Volks convertible—her car. Five years of regular work and when I finally got the divorce I didn't have a penny."

You tell her that was when you found out what it was about. You got wise the hard way. It hurt then, but you are confident that you're the better for it now.

You signal for Stuffy, order, but Carrie won't let you pay. "We split everything," she says. "For the time being we're just partners." She gets her coin purse out. It's one of those old-fashioned coin purses with slots for the different-sized coins. For some reason, it seems sweet to you. You like this girl.

Some loud customers

Three men in satin warm-up jackets come in, carrying plastic bags with their softball uniforms in them. Carol knows one and speaks to him.

"How'd you guys do?"

"What do you think? We start the play-offs next Saturday."

"That is *great*," Stuffy says. "Let me buy you a drink."

He's maybe bought you one drink since you've known him

and he lays out the beer for athletes. Well, what can you expect? He's a team sponsor; he bought three of their uniforms. But why the hell does Carrie act like these guys are pros? She doesn't like sports, never went to enough school to develop an interest in games, which is a sad thing.

"I used to know that guy, he's a nice guy, works for the telephone company, a lineman."

"So?"

"I just said hello to him, Joey. That's all. Listen, let's go. I want to go home and change. I smell from work."

Smell from work has a nice dainty sound to it. "Bring me back something to eat," you say. You give her the key. "There's a rerun of a football game I want to watch."

Games on television

As soon as it starts, you know you watched the original game at home last fall. There's a great pass play in the second quarter, some really beautiful faking by the quarterback and a forty-yard pass. You played a little football in high school. You know how difficult it is to get clear like that halfback did, to take one coming right over your shoulder, especially one that is not thrown high, that zings along hot and flat.

Stuffy buys you a drink. Damn, that's nice of him. Sometimes you forget what a good guy he is; sometimes you tend to jump to conclusions too quickly, to get mad at people for the wrong reasons.

There's a man down at the end of the bar who knows a substitute lineman on one of the teams. All through the game he keeps yelling: "Send in Eddie, he'll show those punks, he's a hard-hittin' son. Eddie's just a little guy, six

six, two forty-three. Just a runt. How'd you like to have that fall on you, huh?"

The trouble with the game now is that the players are freaks, the littlest, lightest players on these squads are horses, or bigger. They would dwarf you. They're monsters, particularly with those helmets that look like business machines and those face guards sticking out. A guy your size hasn't a chance in the game.

"When I was playing ball, we didn't wear face guards." You say that to Stuffy.

You didn't really intend it as a boast. But the guy that knows the sub says: "If you ever got in a game with a bunch of them, you'd need more'n a face guard. You'd need a *body* guard."

Everybody laughs, even Stuffy, and that's what you have come to expect. From everyone. From Carrie as well. People get along well when they get along most of the time. That's the best you can expect from human relations. It's a part-time business, being happy or even relaxed around people. Because, for one reason or another, people don't like each other as much as they let on.

You wish sometimes you read more, books on philosophy and psychology, stuff that explains why people—

"Wow! What a toss!"

"You see the snag!"

That was the pass play. You missed it. They put it on instant slow-motion replay, split screen, but that isn't enough. It doesn't give you the game feeling. Damn, you missed that play. You miss everything. You're a lump, Joe, a dumb lump.

Dolor at the Nitelife

You order another, leave a five on the bar because you trust these people, and go to the can. There's a window open on an air shaft. The walls of the building are gray, so's the exposed plumbing, a rat-colored light there, and it's raining outside. The rain splatters and makes a cold noise that almost chills you.

You wash, look in the mirror, open your mouth and look at your teeth. With your upper lip lifted you remember the time that nut dropped you, and you fold the lip back farther. There isn't even a scar. A fight, you in a fight, for Christ's sweet sake, poor old Joey Beans.

Joey Beans.

You haven't thought of it for years. Mama called you that, during the Depression, when you and the rest of them had to eat so many beans. Your sisters, your brother, and Joey Beans.

That was the best time of your life. Neither Mama nor Dad drank. They were good, they loved you all, they were proud of you, they worked hard. They're dead. And, God, if they knew that you don't see, don't even write, any of your family, now . . . that it is all over, the family, done. Your sister Louise could be dead. You wouldn't know. Your favorite sister. God, what's happened? Have any of them got any boys? Will the name just die out? What *has* happened to you, to that kind of pleasure, to that kind of love? It's awful. It's . . .

Come on, *Joe!* I mean, tears, for God's sake, in a stinking toilet. Tears.

"Hey, how 'bout it Joe? You taking a bath?"

"Yeah, yeah," you say.

You splash water in your face, dry off, go out. You scowl
at Mac. But he bowls you right over with a joke.
"I got a tankful, Joey. I make a mistake and I'll louse up
my tux. I'm on my way to a banquet."
Mac runs the Chevron station down the street. He's in
greasy khaki and he smells of gasoline. A good guy.
The five is still on the bar. Stuffy didn't mix your drink,
but he does so now, as you walk down to your seat. If he'd
mixed it, the ice would have melted. So he didn't, because
he wanted you to have a fresh drink.
One last drink, then dinner.

Mac and Stuffy are both ex-alcoholics
Mac spends as much time in a bar as any drunk, but he
doesn't booze, drinks soda pop. He and Stuffy both have
some funny stories to tell about drunks.
Mac lives in a building with an alcoholic, an ex-lawyer,
who lives with a cat, a black tom. So one day Mac comes in
and sees this guy fallen out of bed, passed out on the floor,
and the cat is sitting on his chest. So Mac pours a saucer
full of wine for the cat, gets him potted so he's howling and
tripping and running into things. Then he wakes up the
guy.
"What'd you do to the cat?" he says.
The drunk sits up, blinks, just as this cat comes tearing
across the floor, jumps over the guy's legs, and lands flat on
his face. The cat screams. The drunk says: "That isn't a
cat. You got d.t.'s, you poor bastard." And he folds up, goes
back to sleep.
Stuffy then tells what it was like when he had this imaginary man following him. He went on month-long drunks,

and at night, when he went to bed, wherever he was staying, there would be this man in the corner of the room. He wanted to fight Stuffy, and all that Stuffy could see of him were his arms, which were big. Stuffy would rise up on his knees in bed, and put out his hands like a boxer, getting ready for the guy to charge.

"But I never swung," Stuffy says, "because I knew that the second I took a poke at this guy, I'd catch myself swinging at the air, and that would be that. I'd feel like an ass. I didn't want to be embarrassed, see, by catching myself doing something nutty. And here I was, drunk as hell, filthy, living like a pig."

You are about to say that pride is one thing a man never loses, when Mac tells another story. He found a calico cat in the yard, brought it into his friend's room, took the black tom out, woke up his friend.

"What happened to your cat?"

The guy began to cry. He cried for an hour. Mac laughs. Stuffy says: "Hell, yes, I believe that. I know what that's like."

He hasn't had a drink since '52. He eats candy, lemon drops. Mac hasn't had a drink in four years. He drinks a case of pop a day.

You aren't worried about becoming a real drunk. You might drop by the Nitelife often, might stay tight over most of a weekend, but you've never gone on a binge, never missed work just because of a hangover, and you've been hitting the bottle pretty hard for quite a while. Stuffy has said as much to you, and he should know.

"If I could've drunk like Joey, here, social drinking, I'd be all right. I really would love to be able to drink now.

But I couldn't trust myself. One jigger, by Christ, and I'd
have to have the bottle. So, nothing since '52.

A late meal at the Nitelife

Carol comes in after the dinner shift. She looks like hell,
and Edith and Charlie are over there, Edith's been looking
at you again, or so it seems. And here comes Carol with a
skirt that hits her in mid-shin and, for God's sake, bobby
sox. She must be the only woman in San Francisco who still
wears bobby sox. The way she dresses and wears her hair
you'd never guess she was still a young woman.

"You get paid?" she asks.

"Yeah, so?"

"Did you cash the check? We ain't got any groceries to
home."

"I'm going out and get a burger," you say.

"Well, I guess I will too, then. First, I think I'll have me
a drink." She starts getting onto the stool.

"Well, look, why don't you . . . ah . . . go on and change
and pick a couple burgers up on the way back?"

"I want me a drink first."

"Oh, want you a drink, huh. Well, I'll get me to ask
Stuffy if you could have you a drink."

You're getting nasty, but, for God's sake, she's so damned
numb she doesn't even know it. Can't tell. God, imagine
what would have happened if the two of you had got
married, like you planned that drunken night, when you
asked Stuffy if he would mind closing the Nitelife for a
party—a wedding party—sometime. You made it sound so
convincing he bought a round of drinks. Thank God he's
never mentioned that.

Carol leaves and comes back an hour later, with a greasy bag—your hamburger. You're dancing with Edith when she comes in. Charlie's right there, so nothing's going on, except Edith feels lighter than any woman you've ever held. (Carol feels like a clothes rack.) Anyway, you're just a little nervous, until you realize Carol didn't go home, didn't change, that she spent the hour shooting the breeze with the cook where she works. The same clothes. The same bobby sox.

"I had my burger there," she says.

"Is there onion on this?"

"Yeah. Go ahead. I had some. Smell." She turns to you, opens her mouth, and huffs out onion smoke. Charming.

You order a beer to go with your meal. She has bourbon on the rocks.

"Sure you don't want water with that?" you ask. If she gets tight now, you'll have to hear about Ben, her first man, and that baby she gave away—the luckiest baby in history.

The lights change

Suddenly you notice the light. The Miller's bouncing color display, and the domed light over the pool table, and the concealed strips of neon behind the bar. Suddenly the light is all you see, and the bottles and glasses and people all look as if they were created by the light, and the light has a sort of power to hold them up, to keep them from falling or disappearing. It feels as if a lot of time went by, but hell, it's only nine or so—ten.

". . . about four years old and he come in with his mama. He was a little devil, that kid. He was dressed so cute, Joey, had real fancy cowboy boots . . ."

You wipe your brow with your handkerchief, and that

moment, when both your hands are off the bar, you feel yourself tipping forward. You reach out quickly, to hold yourself up, and knock your drink skidding. But it doesn't spill.

". . . I says, 'I got a boy your age,' and this little dickens
says, 'I could beat him up,' and he starts in to show me his
muscles. You should've seen him, Joey, he was . . ."

Boy, Joe, it's hitting now. You are getting one big load
on now, Joe. Better ease off.

". . . I couldn't help. I told Lennie I wanted to rest for
a minute, lunch hour or no, because if I didn't I knew I'd
start in to cry out there, and that ain't good for customers
to see. Lucky the boss was gone. But this skinny little kid
looked just like I would guess . . ."

"—will you kindly change the damn record, Carol? Before
I toss my groceries right here."

She says nothing. She leaves.

Right away you know you made a big mistake. But it's been
coming. It had to happen. It isn't even healthy, mentally
healthy, for her to go on harping about the kid, day after
day, every time she gets a drink down.

Stuffy's hands

They're in water so much they have developed a condition.
It isn't very attractive to the eye. The skin flakes off, cracks;
it's a rash. It worries him because he's sure the condition is
caused by the sterilizing solution he has to dip the glasses
into, after washing them. He should wear rubber gloves, but
he can't wear them when the house is crowded, because he
just can't handle orders fast enough if he can't feel the glass.
Without the gloves he's great behind a bar. He can really
move back there.

You see that he's edgy about this rash. He doesn't make enough to hire another barman.

You find it sad. Stuffy is without a doubt the best bartender you've ever met. He can move fast; he knows when to talk; he knows when to shut his mouth. He doesn't make too big a thing of being a reformed drunk. He tells stories about when he was drinking, at least. Not like Mac, who laughs at drunks.

But the condition isn't very pleasant to see, and you would prefer the gloves. Nothing against him, of course. And you know it isn't contagious.

It is later

"Listen, we either dance once more or go now. I got the breakfast shift tomorrow. I'm tired."

Edith and Charlie have left, long ago, so why not? Unless it isn't late; unless she's just trying to haul you away. You bring your wrist up, try to focus on the watch face, curse, then laugh when you recall that there's a huge clock right above the bar.

"Twelve-fifteen! God. I've got work too. I was late once last week. And there's no fooling around on Monday." You rush to the bar, grab up your wallet, cigarettes, change.

"I told you we ought to go to a show. Or spend a night to home. It was you brought us down here."

You put the wallet down. "You know why I didn't spend the night to home, Carol? Because you'd be there! You dumb *lanky, dirty, stupid*—"

"Hey, Joey, take it easy!" Stuffy shouts.

And everybody's listening. Faces turned. Eyes open. Mouth open.

"Man, what an ugly bunch you are. What is this, a local zoo?"

There'll always be friends

"Hey, Joe, haven't seen you in a while."

"I been working. I been around."

"From the looks of you, you haven't missed the bottle. Have you heard from Carol?"

No you haven't. And that's fine. "Yeah, her mother's better. She sends love."

"Hey, Joe," Sammy says, " 'member that Sunday you and me was rolling for beers. Did you notice if I had my watch on? I 'member we were talking about watches or something and I was wonderin' if I took mine off, cause I can't find the damn thing."

"We talked about cigarette lighters."

"Oh."

Molly and Squint don't look up.

"Hiyuh Squint. Hello, Molly, me love."

They nod. All because you told him one night that you wouldn't buy a Buick when, for the same amount of money, you could get an automobile. It was a joke. He'd asked you what you thought of Buicks. Turned out he'd bought one, had it parked outside, and he wanted you to come and see it.

The truth is, you don't care about cars. You're in transportation, right? You dispatch trucks, right? You're around really expensive machinery all the time, so how excited can you get about cars?

You see Charlie down at the end of the bar. Christ. Well, you're in here. Go on. Speak to Louie first.

"Say, Lou, where's your dog? I almost didn't recognize you without that dog."

"I don't want any crap, Joe. I don't have to take that god-damn dog out with me every time I set foot out of the house, and I don't have to take no crap from you or anybody else about it."

"Jesus, Stuffy, you hired you a comedian? Give me a drink, Stuffy." You look now at Charlie. "Can I buy you one, Charlie?"

He sighs, shakes his head. "OK."

You go over, take a seat next to him. "Listen, I been meaning to come and see you and Edith. I'm sorry as hell about the accident, Charlie. I mean words can't express what I feel."

"It's OK, Joe. We all feel bad."

"Edith taking it all right?"

"Nope. She won't hardly say three words a day. She won't eat, she won't sleep. You'd think she was the one driving the car. She cusses herself for buying that bike and, hell, Joe, that bike was around the house for three, four years."

"They still haven't found the car?"

"They won't find it. Cop told me that the other day. Said by now the guy's got the fender straightened, new paint job. They won't find him."

"Gee, I'm sorry, Charlie. Wish there was something I could do."

"Well, if you could bring Edith back to normal, that'd be something. She always liked you. Why'nt you call her?"

Out of the corner of your eye you see Stuffy look up. You know what he's thinking, because it was here that you spoke to Edith on the telephone, right after the little girl was hit, and she had this crazy idea that the reason for the accident was that you and she had been fooling around. She wanted to tell someone—the cops, or Charlie, at least. One day she seemed like the finest woman you'd ever met, even if she was a little older than you, and the very next day she's crazy. It took you an hour to calm her down. And really, you'd be afraid to see her right now.

"Give me another, Stuffy. You want another, Charlie? Give us a couple doubles, Stuffy."

Changes at the Nitelife

You play D-7 and you get loud country music. They've taken off "September Song." Then the television is busted for a week, while Stuffy makes up his mind finally to get color. You alone have paid in enough to buy seven color consoles. At Snavely's, where sometimes you meet Edith, they've got color and wall-to-wall carpeting.

You are almost ready to change, make Snavely's your place, when Edith calls you at work one day and says: "Charlie's sniffing around. He said he won't go to Stuffy's ever again." So you have to settle for the Nitelife.

"Well, damnit, Stuffy, I've had some of the best times of my life here, right here, in this room."

"Sure. I try to make it comfortable."

"What time's it, Stuff?"

"Almost one-fifteen."

"Jesus, gimme a double. I got to leave."

Sometimes you feel like you've got a hollow leg. Sometimes you can drink all night and you're not even sure you'll be able to fall asleep. You forget everything that happens to you until you get to your room, see that nutty little Siamese Edith gave you, and then wake up completely.

"Hey, where's old Mac lately, Stuffy?"

"He went off the wagon, Joe. He's sure to lose his station now. You see, that's the way it is, Joe. There's social drinkers who can take care of themselves. And then there's guys like Mac and me, can't control ourselves. If I took one glass I'd lose my bar."

Closing time

You've bought your last, and Stuff's glancing at you. He's got the gloves off and, God, you have to look away. You're the last customer. He wouldn't show that raw meat to anyone he doesn't know and trust.

You know you ought to leave, but everthing's screwy. You don't even feel tired. Your head hurts, where you fell coming out of the Stardust, where you've started going because, once in a while, some women come there. The pain wakes you up. You think: A nice clean cut on your forehead. More amusement for the drivers on Monday. And Monday is . . . wait, Monday is . . .

"Stuff, this is what? Saturday?"

"You kiddin'? Sunday. You were sittin' right here reading the Sunday paper today when the ball game started."

You giggle. Sunday. Lost a day. "Man, I better haul it. Make a final run to the plumber's and go."

Why do you tell him that? What does he care? He worries about his hands and what happened before 1952. In the can you don't bother to look at yourself. The cut's there. Thank God, Edith will never see that cut, since you won't have to hear how your cut head and the hit-and-run driver and the bike and the dead girl and her rotten parents and Ben are all tied up with the fact that you, for a while, thought you loved her. You splash a little water in your eyes. You don't use a towel. The cool feels good. Your skin burns and you need the cool.

A single woman's come in at this hour. She's down there half-hidden by the rubber plant. Looks all right. Though you can't really see her. But it's late. Come on, Joe, it's almost two. You have four hours, less the time it will take to walk home, to sleep this one off. And you can't miss work. They've given you breaks there; the loaders have covered for you. Come on, Joe, There'll always be women.

"We square, Stuff?"

"Yeah. You better go, kid, it's late."

"Let me buy your most charming customer a final."

"Knock it off, Joe. I'm closing."

"Keeping it for yourself, huh?" You laugh. Stuffy follows you to the door, not for friendship. He has to snap off his neon. He looks very serious. Because of the girl, you think. You step out into slapping cold, hear him lock the door behind you. You start walking, then think of a joke, go back to the door.

"Hey, Stuff! You dirty old bastard! Don't lock that poor girl in there!" You laugh at the idea, bang your fist on the door.

Stuffy jerks the door open, and you damned near fall in on your face.

"Listen, you *bum*, you keep yelling and the cops'll be here! They'll close me up for serving drunks! Now haul it *away!*"

"But what about the girl?"

"What girl?"

You look in, down at the end by the rubber plant. He's right. You would have sworn you saw . . . oh, boy, Joe, are you ever cooked.

You spin around, start down the street. You begin to smile.

It's funny, real funny, that about thinking you saw that woman. That's pretty funny. You'll have to tell the boys about that. You'll have to tell Stuffy. That's pretty damned funny.

CASE

FRANK W.: *The point, here, Mr. Kawnn, is that Ron hired a queer. Maybe not knowingly, though I'm not sure about that, not convinced, but he got a fairy in the office, sir, and how do you think the staff liked using the water fountains after that? I'm not—I hope I'm not—assuming too much when I say that a known fag at the water cooler can kill staff spirit quicker than Asiatic virus. I mean, where's the aspirin and day or two in bed to carry you past that sort of thing. Sure, I'm being vulgar. And I apologize, to Miss Braine and to you, but I'm trying to re-create here an attitude that the employees reflected. I want you to get the feeling, the sense, of this . . . this . . .*

KAWNN: *In your opinion, Frank, this pervert was the first pervert we have had in the shop?*

FRANK W.: *The first obvious one. The first bold one. Rumors crop up whenever there's a bachelor nowadays. But this one didn't introduce any moral doubts to our working community we didn't deserve.*

RUNNING RECORD

Payne Martin Bromley, a slight personage, in dark-blue blazer with silver buttons, gray trousers of a lightweight synthetic, a blue dress shirt, a black knit tie, dark shoes, appeared to be, on the day he applied for the typing job, just a little sporty man with corn-tassel hair. The style of shoes Ron H. admitted he did not note (assumed: they were of a European, probably Italian, make); the blazer was acceptable as apparel, though roughly 78% of all male job applicants fill out the initial application forms in suits, usually dark. Because the blazer was worn buttoned, and the cut was Anglo-American, no comment on the style of the trousers could be made (assumed: they fit tightly). Ron H., assistant personnel supervisor, accepted the ensemble, for he believed all self-supporting typists to be poor. (In fact, he had never before hired a self-supporting male typist.)

Hair color, when broached as meaningful, was summarily dismissed. A personal anecdote submitted by Miss Charlotte Braine (Cha-cha) convinced Mr. Kawnn. She knew, she said, a girl with corn-tassel hair—"golden, lustrous; unbelievable"—and she knew it to be natural.

Payne Martin Bromley, given a few minutes of warm-up, proved himself to be an outstanding typist on electrically or manually operated machines. Accuracy, neatness, speed, speed with figures, and unforgettably swift, accurate, and symmetrical tabulation settings—all were amply in evidence on the tests.

"Best goddamned typist we've ever had here," Ron H. remarked to Miss W., personnel receptionist, who later resigned. Her response:

"Yes, but he's kind of, well, strange, isn't he?"

"Typing's his talent. We need typists."

He was assigned to the typing pool.

Mr. Bromley appeared at work on the second day of his employment in a green check jacket of continental cut and a watermelon shirt. As the tails of the jacket reached just below the waistband of his trousers (the same gray trousers), comment could be made regarding style: Indeed, they were tight. Myers, the office manager in charge of dispatching typing-pool members each morning, brought his daily report to Ron H. with this comment:

"Who's the little flower you sent me?"

"Flower? What do you mean, Myers?" Ron H. asked.

"I mean the little fellow. What are his pants made out of—tape?"

"Bromley. Great typist."

"Anyone can type. He can do more."

Ron's senses were sharp. Question whom Ron employed and you questioned Ron. "What else can he do, Myers?"

"I think he's a queer."

"What's a queer, Myers?"

"A man who likes men."

"Did Mr. Bromley say he liked you, Myers?"

"He's got tape pants on and a shirt the color of lipstick and a green coat."

Myers wore a double-breasted suit coat unbuttoned, so the lapels flapped menacingly, like the wings of a ray fish, when he walked among his underlings. Seldom did pants match coat.

"Is he a queer, Mr. Myers, or does he dress in styles you disapprove of? Shall I call Frank and tell him you want to lodge a complaint against our office because of Bromley's clothes?"

Myers said he didn't like the clothes.

"Thanks for the report."

There were other anti-Bromley remarks made in the first weeks. Ron H. suffered the brunt of them. (So far as is known, Bromley heard nothing directly.) Ron deported himself with professional reserve that no employer could but admire. He knew, of course, that few of the critics had the corporate good in mind. "All gripes merely personal," he noted in a work journal. "Some rather too personal."

Examples of remarks:

Attempted wit (complaint of Jake L., Sales Department): "He's cute, but can he dance?"

Flirtation-inspired (complaint of Nancy Bent, secretary): "Ron, love, I'll get jealous if you bring in competition in stretch pants. I can't wear them here, so I don't have a chance. At home I'm never—well, rarely—out of them."

Neurosis-based (complaint of B. V., respected employee of department that will not be named): "Keep him away from my desk, H., or I swear to Christ I'll smash his dirty little face all over the goddamned toilet."

EXCERPT FROM INQUEST

RON H.: *What I would like here is Frank's comment on B. V.'s remark. Does he agree with that?*

KAWNN: *Keep the private wars out of this. We are talking company, now. Talking years, talking service, morale, perspicacity. Keep the personal junk to a minimum.*

RUNNING RECORD

Ron did not see Mr. Bromley during the first few days of his employment, which is typical Personnel Office procedure.

That the two subjects met in the park is established. The exact date is not known; it is generally believed to have been late in the anti-Bromley phase, when requests for his services were appearing with greater frequency and negative comments were on the decline.

Ron H., in early spring, celebrated the emerging season by purchasing sandwiches—usually white turkey meat, with mayonnaise and lettuce, on plain roll—and milk, and retiring to a nearby neighborhood park, to eat under the trees. (The viands are prepared by Marcus and Sons, Grocers.) Ron H. stood before the meat counter one day in midweek, probably at about 12:05 P.M., and saw a lime-hued shirt, the aforementioned green jacket and gray trousers, and a healthy shock of corn-tassel hair in Marcus' convex antitheft mirror, located over the milk box. Payne Martin Bromley browsed the cookie counter.

Ron H. made no attempt to hail the man. Payne saw him, approached.

"Hi."

"Bromley, how are you?"

"Good, but only because of you."

"Me?" Ron did not feign surprise. He had forgotten the office-gossip factor. (Present-day management must use it in order to control it. Too few administrators realize this.)

"Mrs. Ledesma told me my togs and hair have caused a lot of trouble. And you've stuck by me."

"Well, I've defended my decision as well," Ron said, or has said he said.

Bromley asked if he might be allowed to accompany Ron to the park. Ron assented without pause. ("I couldn't refuse him, though his use of the word 'togs' bothered me, because he was doing well and had obvious need of help. Personnel work isn't buying beef on the hoof, as Frank often says.")

The park was engaged in the transformation expected of parks in spring. That is, there was a resurgence of green—buds, leaves, and so forth. Bums slept on some of the benches. Children played in the sandboxes, on swings, slides, and so forth.

"Do you think my shirts are offensive?" Payne asked, just before tasting his tuna salad on white, the least expensive item on Marcus' menu.

"For certain situations, no. For Kawnn, Incorporated, yes."

"Then why have you stuck by me so magnificently?"

"You represent my decision. I hired you. Also, you have not had time to adjust. I'm sure you haven't been paid yet?"

"I was thinking about asking for special pay. Unless I can borrow some from someone. Stan, my roommate, just started working at a new place too. We're broke. Our rent is—"

"Special pay is available to all new employees." (Ron's inference: This man *is* a faggot. I have hired a homosexual.)

"Anyway, why should I change? Every place I work some Methodist department head, who keeps golf clubs in his office, starts raging about my togs. Or my hair. What's wrong with the way I look?"

The hair, once seen in sunlight, had an almost metallic vibrancy; it threw light but it could as well have thrown heat. ("I was never to know," Ron quipped to an interviewer.)

"What have you done so far, with your bright shirts and . . . and hair?"

"These shirts are handmade. Look at the stitching. They were given to me by a designer who happened to be my size exactly."

A small designer, Ron H. concluded.

"Why should I change?"

"To do better, get ahead, end worrying about being able to pay whatever you owe. Rent. It's a small sacrifice."

"Some of the stuff is old. It was all willed to me by this designer, who killed himself. It has a sentimental value. Billy cut his own throat."

Ron had his pipe out now. It should be noted that he was a recent convert to the pipe. He owned seven, and the usual instruments, including an adjustable reamer. The bitter saliva that collected in the mouthpieces kept him on the verge of nausea most of the time. (He was to throw the lot away after the Bromley incident.) While he smoked, he tipped his head forward to avoid saliva backup. The posture gave him a preoccupied, donnish air. Smoking thus he could not look at those seated at his side, so he nodded sagely. When he spoke he withdrew his pipe, tilted his head back, and seemed to speak with great urgency and amiability. In fact, he was relieved. Had he had the gumption to spit on occasion, he would have been better off.

"You want to kill yourself. You do it when you wear that kind of gear. You get yourself pushed off on the margin of society, where others regarded as freaks collect. It's OK if you can afford it. I couldn't."

"How should I dress?" Payne said, curiously.

"Dress as much like I do as your finances will permit."

EXCERPT FROM INQUEST

FRANK W.: *Teaching him to hide, trick us?*

KAWNN: *Unfortunate.*

RON H.: *I'll bring in the typing tests. I wanted him to adjust. I'll bring in some of the requests for his services that Myers received.*

KAWNN: *Question we must tackle here, lad, is whom you represented. Yourself? Your theories of employment? Or Kawnn?*

RON H.: *They are not distinct.*

KAWNN: *With your permission, I'll reserve judgment as to the benefits to be reaped from such professed selflessness until the present discussion has been terminated.*

RUNNING RECORD

Payne Martin Bromley appeared 16 April in an Arrow shirt —striped, but mildly so. The next day he wore a white broadcloth tab-collar. Following order was established: watermelon, pale blue, peach, Arrow stripe, tab, watermelon, pale blue, peach, etc. A second white shirt replaced the watermelon after the subsequent payday. He bought a dark suit in his second month.

Furthermore, he announced to Ron at one of their meetings in the park that his hair was undergoing a slow alteration.

"Notice anything different?"

"No."

"Hair. It's darker."

Removing his briar so as to look up, Ron said:

"Looks redder, maybe."

"Bronzer. I'm dyeing it back to the normal shade, my shade, by degrees. Stan's helping. He knows hair like nobody I've ever known."

And all the while his typing made him desirable. Jake L., in Sales, sent the following memo to Myers, which Ron presented to all interested parties:

MYERS: Send me the flower on those days when his basic

color does not blind. I will accept him as a permanent typist when his hair reaches shimmering chestnut.

II

RON'S TESTIMONY

(Selected passages with selected interruptions)

Humanistic urges, Mr. Kawnn. The man apart, degenerate if you prefer, comes from the nowhere of an underground existence into the stable, orderly, regimented world of—

KAWNN: Stick to the case. What happened?

He made every effort to adapt. Outwardly, within two months, he was one of us. Better than most. When in the history of the typing pool has a member been singled out and sought after on the basis of his or her proficiency? Granted, young women are often requested by the various departments, but—

KAWNN: The phone call. What happened. Come on. Begin close to the phone call.

FRANK W.: I'll tell you what happened: The flower fell in love with Ron.

MISS BRAINE: *Love? Oh, wow!*

KAWNN: Quit, Cha-cha. Is that true, Ron?

Yes.

KAWNN: Poor devil. Waste. *Waste!*

I had told Bettina about Payne Martin Bromley. We share things. She is going through the period of intensive child care, and most of her hours are taken up with Kaaren, our three-month-old, who is a little colicky. Cries a little. Needs attention often.

Bettina gets bored, worn-out, sometimes thinks she's no kind of mother because she reacts normally, gets angry, feels helpless. It's very difficult to—

KAWNN: Yeah.

It was about this time that Payne and Stan, his roommate, decided to live apart. Payne said it was because he was becoming too conservative for Stan's tastes. I thought that a good sign. Stan had lost still another job in the time Payne had been with us. Payne wanted to find an apartment that was cheap and nearer work. I recommended the area in which we live. East Village, it's called. But it's still the Lower East Side, in terms of rents.

He found a cheap place several blocks from our house. Moved in. We gave a couple of pieces of furniture. He started painting and pulling up linoleum. The smell of paint, and house dust, bothered him. He came to our house a few evenings, at Bettina's invitation, for dinner.

My wife called him. I didn't. All right, she used company time, but they were short calls. She never has much time for telephone calls with Kaaren like she is.

He came, and he was a near neighbor, and Bettina never got to talk to him. Cooking, and the baby, and cleaning up, and boiling bottles took up her time. She took an interest in him. She's a warm, giving person. He—Mr. Bromley— even when his hair was back to normal and his clothes acceptable, had a kind of pathetic way about him. He was little . . . *weak,* we thought, and he had no one after Stan and the dead designer. And we—both of us—showed interest in him. I mean we never reacted negatively when some of the first references to his past were made.

KAWNN: What kind of references?

Oh, just casual things. A party he'd attended. Something a friend said. Nothing too strong.

Anyway, he was happy with us. That's all I can say. One night he told Bettina he was surprised to find that people like us, "straight" people, found him acceptable.

KAWNN: What did your wife say?

She apologized for not being able to spend more time with him.

FRANK W.: Hah! Then who spent the time?

I entertained him, hoping she'd get finished, so she could entertain him. During this period of intensive child care I mentioned, we found we had limited contact with our established friends. Our social evenings were—

KAWNN: OK. OK.

Well, I wanted her to enjoy herself. But she had to devote so much time to the child that she couldn't. I mean, in truth, Kaaren is a very sensitive child, particularly in terms of eating habits. She's a slow feeder, satisfies her sucking instincts on the bottle entirely, and frequently has gas pains, spits up, you know. Also there was heat rash—still is—and a summer cold to contend with.

So I had to handle a lot of these idle moments myself. And I did so by counseling Payne. On the way we—the normal citizens—work. How we adjust to things. How, at times, we adjust our lives to our jobs. If necessary we conceal our feelings in many things, in order to get ahead. I cited the child as an example once. I tried to be frank, told him that, at times, both Bettina and I expressed distaste for Kaaren. In fact, we hated her, I said, which was strong, but I was doing it for an effect. And that we hated spending so many nights alone in the house, rinsing diapers. It's true, Bettina developed a nervous rash on her wrist. She was so sick of testing formula on her wrist that the repulsion she felt eventually expressed itself through this skin disorder. From then on, she had to use my wrist—still does.

But this is off track. The thing that happened was that Mr. Bromley began talking more and more about his past. His family, his boyhood, so on. What you would expect. A classic situation. His mother was a bitch, his father a drunk. She used to set him on the father when the latter came home bombed. Payne'd beat on him. And the father could never recall how it happened. So the mother would invent some persecution the father had perpetrated on them.

He said he became homosexual when he was nine, which I doubt. But there was a story of a boy with a red bicycle. One summer they played in a vacant lot covered with high weeds. They pressed down paths and rooms. He said he fell in love. Or something.

Nothing happened. Fun. It was prepuberty. I can't believe there was much else. All he could remember was that the boy had a ball glove buttoned through his belt loops.

KAWNN: What were your responses to these intimate revelations?

I listened. I was smoking pipes then, having trouble then keeping them lit, and the saliva backup bothered me. I guess I nodded. Sometimes I spoke.

KAWNN: What did you say?

I can't remember. Maybe I said: "Oh, yeah?" Or: "I used to play in the grass." Maybe I compared my boyhood with his. Contrasted, I mean.

FRANK W.: Did you tunnel and make rooms?

Yes. I suppose every boy does that grows up where there are high weeds.

FRANK W.: *I* didn't.

MISS BRAINE: I've heard of it. But I was a girl, never participated.

KAWNN: I never saw a weed till I was twenty-one, and traveling for a dress firm in the Midwest. Go ahead.

Well, he kept telling the stories. He was establishing himself, revealing at my place what he hid at work. And Bettina would come through the living room carrying Kaaren or bringing me a bottle to test, and stop just long enough to get her breath and say something like: "As soon as the baby gets rid of her gas, I'll sit down and maybe we'll have time to talk."

But the baby didn't allow it. Bettina wouldn't use colic medicine, because they contain soporifics. So I listened to the story of his adolescence, high school, the time he tried to join the Army, the business of his piano teacher . . .

MISS BRAINE: Piano teacher?

I'll admit they got a little strong at times, particularly the piano-teacher story. But I thought I was the symbol of respectability to him, so I fought off revulsion. The pipes helped.

One week Kaaren just wouldn't shut up. Bettina was in a frenzy because she'd had diarrhea for two days and she, Bettina, thought it was gastroenteritis. It wasn't, but she went to several pediatricians before she was convinced. That took the edge off her nerves. We were—how shall I say it?—distant. So one doctor prevailed upon her to use the colic medicine, so the baby could have some rest. He in-

sisted the psychological effects of a soporific were no more
indelible than those of three or four nights of hysteria, and
the parents so nervous they could scarcely speak. So we gave
her the stuff. Kaaren went to sleep about seven in the
evening. Bettina and I had a quiet meal. We took cognac
into the living room, stretched out side by side on the couch,
the snifters balanced on our foreheads.

KAWNN: Some kind of sentimental thing?

No, no. It's just that sometimes Bettina and I like to lie
down, side by side, with cognac snifters balanced on our
foreheads. We hold hands and talk about work, vacations,
the future, things. There was still light, and it wasn't too
warm then. It was pleasant.

Then Payne came.

III

UNINTERRUPTED RUNNING RECORD
(*Presented thus for dramatic impact*)

Payne Martin Bromley carried a bottle of California wine
before him. He thrust it into Ron H.'s hand.

"Hi." He walked in. "What's wrong with the baby?"

"She's sleeping."

"Worse?"

"No."

"Where's Bettina?"

"In here," she called from the couch. She had not removed
the cognac. She would have preferred to spend the evening
alone.

They, Ron and Payne, drank an inexpensive mountain
white. Bettina, after complaining to Payne once more that

she was not a good mother, and that she would never have fed her daughter drugs if she were, closed her eyes. She appeared to drowse. Payne apparently saw no reason to alter the course of his evenings with Ron. He soon began an account of what happened to him on one of his first evenings in New York City. (The year of this event cannot be estimated with any hope of accuracy, because Payne had admitted to lying about his age on the application forms at Kawnn, Inc.)

His mother and he had picked out a suit for him before he departed from, let us say, Cleveland. It was a very pale flannel, almost milky, and with it had come a vest. He had bought shoes of gray suède. His shirt was white, his tie a "pathetic" (his adjective) gold.

He went to a party, got up in these traveling clothes. It was here that he met the designer, Billy, but Payne had arrived with some nondescript man of advanced years, a "pickup."

"It was during my kind of awful period, when I just didn't care. Promiscuous. I felt so free. I went with anyone. I was away from that horrible house, that horrible woman. And Dad, who was so weak and sweet. I didn't have to see him destroyed every day."

The party, given by a man who owned three great Danes, was noisy and "fun."

"There was lots of drinking and dancing. Billy was saying that everything was 'pubic' then. 'The pubic moon shines on the public night,' he'd say. He was a riot."

"There were no—ah—women there?" Bettina asked, awake, speaking weakly so as not to shake her glass.

"No, of course not," Ron answered.

"And Stan was there too, though I didn't know it. I just discovered that, recently, quite by accident. I was so—

what shall I say?—overwhelmed, I hardly saw anyone, really. Well, the guy I was with, of course, and Bill, who kept talking about the 'pubic reality.' 'We have to face the pubic reality,' he'd say. 'We're short of drink.' God I miss him, he had the wildest laugh."

"The dogs were there, the Danes?" Bettina asked.

"Yes. They were everywhere. And the guy whose place it was had a fountain, an inside fountain, the first I ever saw, beautiful. With lights playing on the water, cascading down a series of cute things, like shells. Stan and I priced fountains once. We couldn't believe it. Our place had a bathtub in the kitchen, and we were thinking of putting a fountain there."

Bettina sat up, taking her glass from her forehead first, and went to the cognac bottle. She returned to the couch, lowered herself slowly, put the glass back.

"Anyway, someone, and I think it was that devilish Billy, started talking about my clothes. They were horrible, marvelously out-of-town. He started saying things like: 'I never saw anyone look so pubicly white.' And he got the clever idea that I was probably white clear through. Someone said no, I probably wasn't, because no one is completely white—pale like that—all the way through. But Billy insisted. Humorous, of course, he just kept saying that. Pale all the way through. No red meat. A little chicken, he said, without feathers."

"The dogs were just walking around?" Bettina asked.

"They were asleep," Payne said, after pausing to think for a moment. "If you like dogs, Bettina, you'd have loved these. They were extremely gentle, really sweet, but, my God, they were immense. Literally huge."

"She doesn't like dogs," Ron said. "What's this sudden interest in dogs?"

Laughing, Payne told her Billy had a "pubic" idea, suddenly. He wanted to run a test. He asked his friends if they were willing to bet that Payne Martin Bromley was pale all the way down. Some wished to; others didn't. But to test his assertion, Billy suggested they remove Payne's clothing.

"Odd, very odd, and yet . . ." Ron paused, to get the pipe lighter going, "and yet, not so odd. A ritual initiation."

"Would you bring me the cognac?"

"Your glass is still full," Ron said.

"By the time you bring me the cognac, it won't be." She was right. Ron had to pour carefully. A splash in her eyes would have been painful.

"So, first thing I knew, Billy came up and took off my tie. Then someone unbuttoned my jacket and took it off. 'White vest,' they all shrieked. 'White shirt. Billy's winning.' "

They began to strip him. He alone, a confused but elated "Cleveland" boy, stood in the center of a group of perfect strangers "laughing my head off." They pushed him into a chair to remove the shoes. They stood him up to get the shirt off.

"White T shirt. Arms of a pubic blue-white."

"What did the dogs do?"

"They slept," Ron H. said, speaking rather abruptly. He had heard stories like this before. To listen to them, he kept lighting the pipe, never interrupted, and imagined Payne Martin Bromley's hostility toward the normal—in his words, "straight"—world was diminished by every phrase.

"What do you know about it? Maybe they were killing someone."

"They were gentle. They slept along the wall that led to

the kitchen, curled against the baseboard. You could hardly pass between the sofa and the wall. But they never bothered anyone."

"So it went on to its obvious conclusion, eh?" Ron said, chuckling, moving things forward, as he did sometimes.

"Yes, in a few minutes I was standing there in my undertogs, and they were all yelling, and Billy was going around telling everyone to get their money ready, and—"

"Surely," Bettina said, sitting up again, holding her glass beneath her mouth. "Surely to Christ they could tell by then, couldn't they?"

"By then," Ron interjected, "the pseudo-formal reason for the investigation had probably been forgotten, hadn't it? I mean, there were fewer references to the color of your skin and more—"

"More pubic stuff," Bettina said, standing up. "I wish I had been to that party. As a great Dane. I'd have killed the whole bunch of you. Including you."

She left the room.

EXCERPT FROM INQUEST

KAWNN: *Pardon me for nosing about like this but why, in the name of God, would you interrupt what must have been a romantic situation and rise from a nesting place of such serenity, abandoning your wife, whom I've never met but am convinced is a gem, to throw open the door to a sexual insect like that?*

FRANK W.: *Maybe he wanted—*

RON H.: *Listen, Frank, I'll kick your teeth down your throat if you make one more remark like that. Job or no job.*

KAWNN: *Seven years here, boy. And what sort of recommendation could you get? You got a wife, a kid. Security*

*is the watchword in the modern age. Better prove your
case.*

UNINTERRUPTED RUNNING RECORD (CONT.)

"I'm sorry," Payne said. "I never know how to talk to
wives."

"Neither do husbands, most of the time," Ron said. He
rose and went to the fireplace, where he knocked out his
pipe. "We've got to be careful always what we say to people.
A story like this would get you fired in a minute. Not everyone would understand the ritualistic demands of your, shall
I say, mode of existence. Some would isolate this situation,
generalize from it, rather than take into account your recent
progress toward a less blatant form of expression."

"Only you understand, Ron. And I'm so lonely now. I
don't want to start cruising again. But I'm so lonely. God,
I hope I can talk to you some more. I hope I haven't ruined
everything between us."

"Anything you could ruin has to have a reason for being
vulnerable. If it happens that Bettina and I have a rift, the
trouble was always there, but we kept it hidden. That's the
way things are. There's always trouble, but you keep it hidden. But I think it would be better if you didn't come
around for a while."

EXCERPT FROM INQUEST

FRANK W.: *I suppose you said that to help him?*
RON H.: *Yes.*
FRANK W.: *While your wife was in the next room, crying her
eyes out, insulted, feeling filth had crept into her house.*
RON H.: *She was sleeping. She slept eight hours that night*

and the next morning she woke up feeling she'd been wrong to treat Payne like that.

KAWNN: Why?

RON H.: Because I reminded her that we have always made it a habit to be understanding, Mr. Kawnn. Payne Martin Bromley was . . . well, whatever you want to call him, he was a human being. He couldn't change what circumstances had forced him to be. He was homosexual. I felt sorry for him, during that period.

KAWNN: And your wife felt sorry too?

RON H.: For as long as either of us did. Which amounted to about two weeks, until the telephone calls began.

TELEPHONE CALLS

(One sample from each of the three marked phases)

Example of calls in first phase:

PAYNE MARTIN BROMLEY: Ron? It's me, Payne. Can we talk a minute? I've been thinking. Bettina just ruins our meetings for us. I mean, we can't hide everything, all the time. You come to my house at nine tonight. OK?

RON H.: What the hell are you talking about?

PAYNE MARTIN BROMLEY: You won't have to conceal anything at my place.

Click. Connection broken by Ron.

Example of calls in second phase:

UNIDENTIFIED TENOR VOICE: You miss me, don't you? I miss you. I keep it hidden, and even if it's just a spiritual kind of thing, I love you—

Click. Connection broken by Ron.

Example of calls in final phase:

UNIDENTIFIED VOICE (*almost incantatory in effect, as if speaker is "under the influence"*): I love you. I don't give a damn. I love—

Click. Connection broken twice by Frank. (Ron hung up third time.)

EXCERPT FROM INQUEST

FRANK W.: *That's what I heard. Jesus, that's it. Picked up his phone one day. Heard it. Couldn't believe. Thought I was dreaming. Same call next day. I heard. Sick.*

UNINTERRUPTED RUNNING RECORD (CONT.)

Ron told Bettina. Fortunately, all this occurred when, effects be damned, she was giving Kaaren the colic medicine regularly. Bettina, in turn, was well rested, felt better all around, and understood her husband's trepidations: the operators who overheard; the way gossip spreads; the trouble that could arise if steps weren't taken. She knew, shared, Ron's concerns, even accepted some responsibility.

"I've drawn away from you, to motherhood, which I'm a flop at. I haven't done enough, helped you. I will now."

She called the office the next day, spoke to Payne, told him he was missed at the H. house. "Ron needs you, Payne. You've proved his theories. And now he's troubled. Come after dinner, tonight, at—say—nine. He asked me to call."

Briefing Ron as to what she planned presented certain difficulties. He resisted her tactic, declaring it inhuman. She had to stress the seven years at Kawnn, Inc., Kaaren's possible orthodontic problems, a "reasonable" life insurance. Kaaren's education, other things. Ron H. came around to her way of thinking by nine.

EXCERPT FROM INQUEST

KAWNN: *It was all her doing?*

RON H.: *No, sir, I agreed to her proposal. My agreement was my doing.*

FRANK W.: *Did you agree readily?*

KAWNN: *Come on, Frank. He agreed. Cut the CIA crap.*

UNINTERRUPTED RUNNING RECORD (CONT.)

Payne Martin Bromley arrived at the appointed hour, wine outthrust. But the door was ajar. His knock pushed it open.

Two voices in unison called out: "Come in." The voices were those of Ron and Bettina, issuing from the couch.

Glasses on foreheads, they waited. Ron was tense. Bettina as well.

"Hi," said Ron, without rising.

"Hi," said Bettina.

"What's going on?" asked Payne Martin Bromley. (Assumed: he was confused.)

The glasses were more than half empty. By squeezing Ron's hand, Bettina indicated that she was ready. Both sat up, downed the contents of the glasses, put the glasses aside, and lay back down.

"I hope I'm not bothering you guys . . . I . . ."

Ron rolled over on his side, facing his wife. He lifted his uppermost leg and draped it, ceremoniously, across Bettina's calves.

"Hmm?" Bettina inquired.

"I was saying I . . ."

"Baby," Ron whispered, as planned.

"Oh, yes," she exclaimed, ecstatically. She kissed him. Payne Martin Bromley left then.

He has not been heard of since.

EXCERPT FROM INQUEST

KAWNN: *God, what a woman. She reminds me of—*
FRANK W.: *But, but—I don't believe it.*
RON H.: *Search my house. Ask Bettina.* Come on, all of you
—you too, Miss Braine—come to my house, meet my
wife, my baby, have a drink. Ask.
KAWNN: *That's a remarkable woman you've got there H.
I'll want to sleep on this tonight, but you can tell her for
me I find her admirable. Guts, you know. Real guts.*

IV

MR. KAWNN'S SUMMARY AND JUDGMENT
(*Entire section was tape-recorded. The speaker was called
away on business. Miss Braine was present at the recording
session and the playback.*)

The story of this unnecessary, squalid youth who penetrated
an organization some have called mighty with his poisonous
frivolity reminds me of something from my past. Particularly
am I drawn back by the contributions of Ron's wife—she
saved your neck, boy, in more ways than one. Take her a
gift. Flatter her. She deserves flattery. Among all the multitude of women with which I have at one time or another
had my way, purchased or gratis, I have failed to flatter only
one, the gentle Evie. And in the stupefying act of negli-
gence I shrank my heart three sizes, lost the angelic creature,
and became what you saw before you yesterday. A fat, sensu-
ous gaffer with a stomach like an old tire and a fading
Miami tan.

Don't call me Boobie, Cha-cha, and don't try to reassure. You know the truth like no one.

I turn the clock back thirty years. I ask you all to peer

with me toward a small galvanized-iron shack beneath the Williamsburg Bridge approach, and into a small apartment, now vanished, on the Delancey Street that is southernmost, near the corner of Columbia. Today children play in that area, and old men deal pinochle under the trees, waiting for the end. And all that remains of the past is the bridge itself, the poultry market, the fetid public toilets. Thirty years ago in that single block of this tumultuous metropolis were established the poles of my existence, settled forever, as if by the hand of God. Evie on one end. Work on the other. Barely fifty yards separating.

I recall the notes she would write to me late, late at night, after the skimpy meals, after she had tidied up, after indulging ourselves in the delights of the flesh. "You big devil," she'd say, "what did you make me do? I love you beyond words." I made her do nothing. That was her way —playing, playing. Hair that never smelled of food, but of the sweet, wide, windswept American prairies, from whence she came. Arms white as milk. Nipples like clusters of raisins. My God, look at me and laugh.

I slept, tired beyond dreams, the sleep of a dray horse. I ate. I loved. But I worked, and work like you've never seen done. I was young. Independent. My parents in their graves. My one sister married a dentist. She took riding lessons in the park every morning, talked about AT&T like it was something she cooked in her kitchen. I was independent, except for the tin shack under the ear-splitting bridge. I never saw sunlight. I knew noon by the jar of chicken soup Evie brought and left inside the door with another note. I knew winter when the freezing air whistled through nail holes in the tin.

Years passed, and in the nights, late, I ran up three flights to find Evie waiting at the door in her better dress, in what we called her "glad rags." She thought she was hippy; gentlemen, the women we love are never fat.

"Si, take me to the Copa?" she asked, as I came home. "No? Then come in. It's specials and beans, your favorite."

Did I feel anything amiss? How could I? Love was my mirror. My health I thought was a gift. Tired? Sluggish? Who was less? That was the decade without weekends, the thirties. She got me up in the morning, so worn I couldn't remember, and she had the lather and a warm cloth prepared. She led me, blind and wheezing with sleep, to a chair, shaved me, combed my hair, forced the roll and coffee down me. I have had great barbers since. Barbers of senators, movie stars, Italian gangsters. None fails to nick me on the ear lobe every third or fourth shave, due to an unusual beard configuration. She did not. She had surgeon's grace with that straight razor.

She dressed me as well. She led me to the street.

You all smile, I suppose. Yes, it's touching. But it ended. I began to succeed. It had to pay, all that labor, in some way. Money was the expected tender. I thought for a while it was the only one. One afternoon I shut the tin shack for the last time. I spat on the window, spat on the door, spat in the guts of the padlock, and moved uptown. Bigger floor space, a colored man helping, pipes and running water in the back room, the first telephone I ever operated. I was twenty-seven years old—your age, Ron—and sick as hell and didn't know it. How did I find out? I told Evie I wanted to wear a tie to work.

"No," she said. "The old open collars are the best. No constriction."

"A tie, now. I'm a boss."

"Si, for my sake, no?" Our first disagreement. It was hardly a fight. Only, I had to walk to Clinton to buy the shirt. The man took one look at me and said: "With a neck like that the arms aren't going to fit." Neck? I queried. It's the same old stem, is it not? I stepped before his mirror. For the first time I paused, momentarily, to regard the man I had become. I staggered from the shop of that Clinton Street clothier a moment later, aghast and incredulous. I was a freak.

A goiter, gentlemen! A bulbous growth. Suddenly I'm a thyroid case, with another head shoving its way out of me. I ran home.

I burst into our apartment. She was waiting. I said: "Look, Evie, look! But don't touch. What is that business?"

"Si, it's been there," she said, calmly.

"Been there? Then I ain't."

"You ain't been wearing ties."

"Why didn't you tell me?"

"Because you had things to do. Because it didn't make any difference."

"To you? No difference living with Jo-jo, the two-headed wonder? What do I mean to you? What do you mean to yourself? Overnight I become funny-looking in a very unhealthy way, and you say it means nothing. What is your interest in this swelling, Evie? What psychological manhole did you fall in? An enormous goiter, for the love of God. What am I, suddenly, Siamese?"

The beginning of the end, gentlemen. I was sailing away from joy on a sea of thyroxine. My hands shook. I noticed for the first time, I paused to notice, my nauseating eyeballs, which defied the laws of gravity by remaining stuck to my head. They bulge today; and don't deny it, Cha-cha. But I've had treatment. Then, under the totalitarian secretions of a single gland, they appeared to be defecting from my body, seeking independence.

I will condense what followed. Shame forces me to shorten it. I blamed my Evie, not the unforgivable gland. I learned vanity in an instant. I said: "You could have saved me from this unwholesome appearance, Evie." She said: "I love you, Si. What's more wholesome? You were bothered enough by work." I accused her of impeding my humanity, my progress. "A runaway thyroid wears a person out, steals his energy, renders him offensive to clients, makes him a visual cripple. My work? Were you thinking of it? Were you thinking of anything when you said nothing?"

"I didn't know you cared, Si."

Her ignorance of the inner workings of the human body staggered me, as did her innocence of matters mental. Her bland acceptance of my deformity made me doubt her mind. She was pretty. Could a totally pretty girl live with a goiter? Love it? Shave it?

Clinics, operations, time off in the day, to be made up by long hours at night, and a great mistake, a rest-room mirror, which I put in the back, changed my life.

I began to study myself like a scholar. This nose, no beauty, and don't lie, Cha-cha, was for me at first grotesque. But later I saw in it what I guess these jackasses with ropes see when they crawl up the side of dangerous mountains at enormous personal risk. I saw a natural disturbance over which a measly man has to triumph in order not to believe that nature comes first, dominating the order of things. There are the forces of nature; then there are the forces of the mind. I wanted mind first. Because I was the proprietor.

With the help of the doctors I broke the back of the

goiter. Under the onslaught of medical wizardry, the gland retreated. With scholarship I reduced to an abstraction this nose. From that point on, gentlemen, the world became a puzzle which I put together at great profit, speaking monetarily. But I lost my golden girl.

Why did she go?

I drove her out.

How?

I couldn't see her. As my eyes snuggled back into their sockets, my eyesight changed. What was one day whole, a solid, sweet-skinned entity, became, the next, a series of parts. I turned my scholarship on them too. I began to ask questions of myself and of her.

How long can a beautiful, loving girl eat chicken soup, cook it and eat it, always carefully keeping the odor of food from her hair, and not strangle? How long can she share a dreary apartment, her sole recreation shopping and a little, untiringly sexual man who comes home at the odd hour with his various appetites raging? Of what universal meaning are a few faded print dresses, bought from the handcart, when there's money in the bank? And she was free to take all of it, gentlemen, always. What was the Copa of her fantasy, where we were never to go? Or were we there?

Who was this girl, I asked myself, this female problem?

And she became just that. A problem. I came home to her. I loved her. We played our tricks. But I kept asking why? Why does she like me? Why does she like how we love? Live? Eat? Never dance? Hurt ourselves with work?

"Why?" I would ask.

"You know," she'd say. "If you don't know, who can? Eat your special, Si, don't ask so much. You make me feel like a bug."

"Why? Why should I eat rather than talk?"

"Well, one reason, Si, is because you get something in return for eating."

"Why must I have returns?"

On. On. Finally, she was saying: "No more questions, please." And I wanted to know why. Then she was saying nothing. And again I wanted to know why. Then she was gone, one day, and her final note stated, in the simplest terms, the only answer she ever gave me. The only answer she had.

"Love."

Since then, gentlemen, I have enjoyed myself with a series of tall, fleshy women who, more often than not, have altered the color of their hair, who frequently have been married on more than one occasion, who supply my needs without restraint, and know how to enjoy themselves. I have had fun. I have always been generous in my recompense. Not a few of their kids have I put through college. I pride myself on saying that I have fostered good feelings and honest pleasure. But I have not recovered love, and this is no insult to Cha-cha or to the others. I cured myself of a nasty thyroid condition and tendency toward simple belief in people. Even more simple than that, for the word belief did not occur to me. Love was there. I had it. When it was nameless.

MR. KAWNN'S APPLICATION OF ANECDOTE TO INQUEST

The reason I have broached this circumspect tale of my personal cataclysm is severalfold. I will now attempt to relate the matter to what we are dealing with:

First: I see Frank like I was with my goiter, in the winter of our—Evie's and my—relationship. Full of hatred for what seemed betrayal. But ask yourself today where is this social blemish—this boy, Paine Bromley? Molesting our equipment? Defiling our typing pool? Is he walking in your midst with no clothes on?

Second: I see in Mrs. H.'s clever and bold solution Evie's attempt to keep me away from the shirt shop. Thank your stars, Ron, that you took her advice.

Third: I see in both of you the old urge to conquer worlds, even if it means shedding blood. A feeling, gentlemen, which came, I swear, to me only after I was bereft of my golden girl. Before that I worked at a certain rate for the same reason I breathed at a certain rate, because I knew that was what man did to stay alive. I will tell you in a few moments why this is ridiculous.

We have dealt with elements which make our world: social order, human relationships, the decline of trust. I would like to discuss these things now, each in its place.

In the first place, I too was a freak once, man apart, and with determination, I rose above the gross imperfection to whatever position I have now achieved. So I am hesitant to share an intolerant attitude toward the hapless pervert. If the boy's trouble were gland precipitated, Frank, would you hate him? Do you hate the halt, the hunched?

In the second place, love is a cherished memory for me. And however repulsive the boy's affections for Ron may be, I am not able to relinquish my respect for the feeling, which, in both cases mentioned here, may have been absolutely ill-founded, but did not involve sacrifice, did survive many staggering thrusts of brutish minds, and remained intact longer than any other feeling alluded to in this inquest. Except suspicion, which is the pig in the poke today.

For we are here, gentlemen, in the third place, to celebrate suspicion. Thus to manifest our distrust of our fellows. Two people whose names have figured prominently in this discussion did not distrust. Are they any worse off, any more misguided, any more discomfited by accusations, insights, uncovered fears than we? This I doubt. Look at you, Frank. Shriveled because a pip-squeak tells you he loves you? By mistake. Look at Ron, giving what he thinks is profound advice to the same pip-squeak, and discovering finally that all he said was twisted by this kid into a kind of love poem.

You suspect yourselves, others. How does this happen?

Where does suspicion rise? In that chamber of the heart vacated by love, when it was dug out by the roots, by selfishness, vanity. It grows like fungus, gentlemen, suspicion does. This corporation, which some call mighty, is a circus of suspicion now. In the tin shack, it was in that regard, a monk's cell. I let it happen. It's what happens when there are problems.

The tape recordings, the interviews, the secret files, the defensive files, this makes me want to puke my guts up, because it is mine, and I am the father of it, and, even now, in a moment when I hear of some kind of deviation from the norm, I allow such a hearing to take place. Because I distrust.

But in my heart, gentlemen, I retain a smattering of the old respect for good food, hard work, physical diversion, and trust. And love echoes there. And I don't give a damn about immorality infecting everybody, Frank, because it's here anyway. Only by luck, sometimes, a being escapes it for a while, with the help of another, usually a woman, but . . . who knows?

The case is dismissed. No action to be taken. Forget it. Forgive. Shake hands, you two. See to it, Cha-cha. And allow me one prediction. The day is coming when success, theory, ambition, cutthroat effort will be like so much water off the back of an electronic duck. So forget and forgive. Your time is fast fading, both of you. Work hard, without aggressing between yourselves before you become phased-out dross, impeached by progress, retired in your mid-forties. Before you face a prospect of endless recreation —tennis, the trailer house, the camper's stove that never lights.

I am an old man, barely over five foot tall, with legs thin as pencils, netted with veins, and a waist size that is only comic. Hundred fifty-eight, by my own scales, this morning. I got a scar on my neck; my eyes water day and night. My hair looks like lint you find in rolls under your bed. I haven't had a tooth of my own since before you were born, Ron. Remember me. Remember what I look like. I'm your leader. I could fire you both right now. Ruin you. You like that? No.

And don't deny, Cha-cha, don't shake your head; you don't like this hull any more than I do.

But I will tell you something, all of you. I am a man, the best goddamned thing that ever happened to the earth, and I am still a man, no matter how I look, and it is from such a small compound of ugliness and energy that all your best conclusions have to be drawn. There's nobody else.

RESULT OF MR. KAWNN'S SUMMARY AND JUDGMENT

1. Ron H., Frank W., and Miss Braine applaud at length. [The three turned to face the tape recorder. It is agreed that the applause might have been longer in duration had the speaker been present.]
2. Ron H. and Frank W. shake hands, pat each other.

3. All return to work.
4. (After some delay) Ron calls Bettina: "It's OK, baby. The sonafabitch couldn't make it stick. But I'll get him for this, I swear to God, I'll get him. . . ."

CASE CLOSED

DOG

Roi got sick while I was combing my hair over the kitchen table—yesterday's *Times* opened to the ads. I heard his claws clicking out in the laundry space, where he sulks or muses. I paid no attention until he came in. He coughed, a few plain coughs; then gagging, then spine-bowing heaves. He threw up, a small bilious spit, almost clear. He looked at the wet, then at me.

"Oh! I'm sorry," I said.

I gave him bread—old bread—in a bowl of milk, which he enjoys in the morning, and which I had forgotten that day. I blamed my house guest, Myra, still sleeping.

Cleaning it up, I took tissue, wiped up the mess, making three trips to the bathroom. The floor was dry, not clean. Flushing was a problem. Myra slept in my daughter's room, on the other side of the toilet, and my plumbing whines and sings. In the mornings I preferred her asleep; in the afternoons, shopping; in the evenings, out. She had just left her husband, who was my friend. But sheltering a deserter is usually taken seriously. It wasn't important, but I hated it, and her for it, somewhat, I suspect.

She woke up anyway and came to lean on the doorframe, face swollen, eyes just starting into sight, a milky morning film on her teeth and lips. She smacks gravely, over and over, first thing in the morning. She crossed her arms before her, snuggling up for the warmth, fluffing out small breasts.

I would have said nothing but she began a dull amble to the refrigerator for orange juice, slapping her bare feet. That walk would have taken her near the spot Roi dirtied. I thought of worms, parasites that enter through the soles of feet, that you do not forget from zoology class. So I told her.

She scolded him, sweetly. "You are sick inside and dirty out, Roisie. You have an awful smell and an upset stomach." She stopped over him, her head shaking. Cute.

It was a bad job. Roi didn't give her a nod. He maintains a preposterous dignity still. At nine, having lived too long, fat, and more sheep than poodle in appearance now, he is my willing representative. Myra tried smiling at me, but received little in the way of recognition, and so retreated for slippers with unfortunate, high-lifting knees. I did this for her: I poured her orange juice, heated the coffee, prepared her toast. And I removed the newspaper and emptied the ashtray in which I placed the hair that comes out.

She sat down, yawned several times. She had not washed her face well before retiring. Green eye shadow lurked in a fold of her right eyelid. She ate slowly, making dry noises with her toast. Her bites were always too large; she could not close her mouth over those bites, so the toast broke up noisily, and I went through each stage with the toast. She was chewing on my bones. She could have moistened it, eased things somewhat.

"I talked to George last night. He said you were going to see his friend tomorrow—today. Is that right?"

"At eleven-thirty."

"You didn't mention it yesterday."

"No. Would you like more coffee? That toast must be very dry."

She does have fine shoulders, high-school swim-team shoulders. Her nightgown was loose. Along the marked serrations curving on her curved spine, I could almost feel a forefinger bouncing. Up and out along the muscular shoulder, pressing bone and skin, back to the tendons at her neck and up under her chin, where she would still be warm and damp with sleep. There to pinch her until she shrieked. (Sometimes I get dizzy, thinking that I think like that.)

"If you really want help, George is the one to help. He knows everything, everybody."

"You always feel that way about lawyers now. You love them. They listen to you and believe you."

"He wants me to go back to Peter if I possibly can."

"You couldn't do that, though," I said. I did not mean to sound patronizing, but that note comes readily at times. At times I don't realize I've adopted it.

"You're mad because I told George you read the ads? Nina, I was trying to help. You've helped *me. Enormously.*"

"Yes."

George was her lawyer, a professional scattergood with the tousled hair and tight suits. He chortled and called us all "you gals." Myra mentioned one night that my husband's—the second's—attorney had written concerning the size of my alimony and the use to which I put it, enclosing an unveiled threat to my way of life. So George started assuring me. California was one of "you gal's states." "Don't fret yourself, Nina," he said. I thought "fret" well chosen. Apparently a lot of Manhattan women with hyper-urban ambitions take strength from his barney style—a Harvard Law redneck in big, scuffed shoes. He said I didn't have to *wuck*. But if I *wantid* to *wuck* he'd look aroun' fer somethin'.

"After today, I won't bother him. Or you." It sounded a bit harsh. I smiled; affirm the instant. "I'm going out for the newspaper and mail. Do you want rolls?"

No. Thanks.

II

In telling all about my economics I include this: I am almost a landowner. With someone, I signed a contract to pay for a narrow brownstone on Twelfth between Second Avenue and Third. Four floors, walk-up, on each floor a good-sized flat. I live on the street level, in what must have been the basement once, for the odd shape of it. It's dark, locks up tight, and is a good place to leave, walking a dog.

A man comes by mornings to rattle garbage cans and clean the sidewalk of liabilities. He wears starched khaki and polished, high-top shoes. The fading blue verge of a tattoo peeps occasionally from beneath a rolled sleeve. He isn't young; and he's the super of a neighboring apartment house. There is about him an oppressive immaculateness—the wearying aroma of shaving lotion, freshly applied. He cuts his hair so plenty of scalp shines. I believe he is retired Armed Services, but he could be a clean alcoholic.

He whistles show tunes, calls me Nina.

"Bob," I said, that morning.

"Nina."

Walking away, I wandered with his eyes over my thinness,

as I followed Roi's surges at the leash, thinking: I'll have trouble with him someday. Which was nonsense.

No letters, I add. I look for two when I get mail. One is from my daughter, this term in love with a science teacher and flunking her other classes. Last year it was history.

The other is from a man—very rich, older than Bob, but not retired. He lives in Puerto Rico and owns five small hills covered with sugar cane and a share in the mill that refines it. Once he flew me over the hills and I asked: "What's yours down there?" "That," he said, and made a substantial swipe with his hand. So I said: "I'll marry you. I'm a friend of the hill."

He laughed, but I'm happy I made that proposal after we bought the house. He provided the down payment, which I pay back in regular monthly installments.

He's good, builds houses down there. And he writes excellent letters about the slums—El Fanguito and La Perla. He tells me about filth and rats and various resident stinks. He wants to replace all with low-cost, efficiency housing. I think that is aim enough. I tell him that and then sneak in questions about electrical fixtures and plumbing problems. So, on occasion, I have received crated toilets and rolls of wire at my door. And the apartments get better.

On that day, no letters. Nothing.

I walked, and it was pleasant walking on Second Avenue. I bought bread at Ratner's bake shop and the newspaper from outside a Ukrainian café. Coming back the city felt good. A sky the color of day-old snow and a low mean wind snapping at the ankles. The buildings, black and staggered, looked impossible to inhabit, and winter raced out of the intersection, out from Brooklyn and beyond.

In New York you always have a sense of what you have
survived, what's upcoming.

I skidded behind Roi until he quit pulling. That happens
about halfway back. He fails physically; he continues to sniff
and casts robust barks when other walked dogs appear, but
that's just his undaunted spirit.

Myra had just stepped out of the shower. She confronted
us in her underclothes. She held a new evening wrap, the
first fruit of her freedom, muscatel-colored outside and with
what should have been white lining. There were cloudy
smudges. Roi trotted off to the kitchen, dragging his leash.
He accepted his guilt. But he is a fat, castrated poodle living
in decadence, and he could be as trite as his circumstances.
He hid in a corner where I had placed two empty bottles of
Chivas Regal that should not have been empty. I buy my
drinking whiskey from Macy's. The labels are curious but
the price is right.

"You can't leave good clothes around. He loves the smell
of your flesh."

"Don't they launder capitalists' pets? Pick up and deliver
in Cadillacs or something? He needs professional help."

"They charge too much. And they are nuts, the people
who do that. I'll get your coat cleaned. I'll take it in this
afternoon. I would now but I'm tied up this morning."

I used the wrong tone of voice.

"I knew you weren't serious. George swears that in California, girls like us are—"

"I'm going. You can help me by keeping my dog. If you
won't beat him."

"Nina, you've got to admit he smells. He's dirty. It can't
be healthy. For *him*. And the whole house . . . well, I'm in

no position to complain. You've saved my life, you know.
You and dirty ol', sweet ol' Roisie."

III

As character references—an ash-colored suit and one of my
daughter's blouses. Medium heels, sturdy and sensible,
polished by hand before the dog got sick. (I rise very early
and wander about the apartment with the lights off, the
radio, a large, luminous German set, tuned in to a Sybaritic
station in Jersey. All of predawn Manhattan is bathed in
tangos and sweet, empty waltzes.) I wore my hair like Alice
and Eustacia Vye. (Someone named Richter, Mr. Hardy
tells us, said: "Nothing can embellish a beautiful face more
than a narrow band drawn over the brow." I read it young,
memorized it, believe it still.)

My last husband, during the decline, summed me up
neatly once, after I'd stood for an hour on the terrace of our
Hyde Street apartment, looking at Alcatraz swim through
a fog.

"You're like a cat watching a fly outside the window."

That's the way: catlike, thin and long; and that's the way
I act.

I cabbed it, planning to return on foot no matter what
the weather. Tulio Ghardelli drove, and not too happily, for
the trip was short. Rolling in the warm taxi across town, and
getting warm in woolens, I sneezed twice. Once more, and I
would have gone back. But, no.

Tulio, not even courteous considering the undeserved tip,
dropped me, without quite stopping, before Schrafft's on
Thirteenth and Fifth Avenue. There I had coffee, for I was
early, and got dismally nervous. Schrafft's fed light snacks to

ladies from the residential hotels along lower Fifth—olive eaters, black pits on every saucer. In one of the two trips to the rest room I interrupted a bold matron rinsing off her upper plate. She appeared calm; she regarded me with an impassive if sunken mouth through the mirror. I might have been sick had she not shown such resignation. They do not often feed the frantic there, at that hour.

Finally, I walked down three blocks to a morose old brownstone with a wrought-iron symbol above the entrance —twisted initials in art-nouveau curlicue—and old, revolving doors. Inside, there were portraits of "our authors," most of them dead, lining the walls. Mrs. Sullivan, a sincerely cheerful receptionist, did me no good. I wanted disinterest or worse. I would one day have her fired.

The elevator was perfect, old wood paneling and plenty of warnings posted. The operator prevented me from tapping and hiking at my clothes. I did take a dozen deep breaths while we swayed and rattled upward.

Then there was a field of cells, topless, formed of metal-and-scratched-glass partitions. None of the messy-desked girls with the publishers' accents knew precisely where Mr. Flannery was located. The gum-chewer from Brooklyn said: "Third on the right. The big guy with the cold."

Behind a doorless opening, then, a book-lined dead end. Scene of an entertaining decline.

IV

"Mr. Flannery? I'm Nina Ward."

"Cub id," he said. He shifted a wad of Kleenex from right to left hand and passed the infection over. From then on I swarmed with microscopic life. Otherwise he was inappropriately handsome, save for the seared nostrils and wet eyes. (But, I supplied, just a *trifle* effeminate?) We mentioned our friend-in-common. George had helped him out with a legacy problem once. Hardly involved enough to be worth George's time. Still, he worried over the principles. That was his decent way.

"George is fine, one of the best," I said.

I stood betimes, thinking a chair would bring composure. I sat down and fell all apart.

I won't try to maintain his afflicted speech; Mr. Flannery does not star here. Begin, in the next paragraph, was "begid"; telling was "teddig." And so on.

"I'll begin by telling you what I function as here," he said. "That will get us off to a realistic start. I'm not in a position to hire you. I occasionally hire assistant editors for the College Text Division, but at present I don't need anyone. I may be able to put you in the way of another opening, in another division. I can recommend you. If you're interested."

Something like that. To which I nodded promptly. I felt a little relieved and began scratching my chin. I caught myself at it and jerked the hand down so it struck my bag a cannon clap. Flannery, rummaging a drawer, looked up and blinked the weary eyes.

"I had a set of applications sent up from personnel. If you . . ."

"I was thinking about fiction. The fiction department. Fiction would be the sort of thing I think I'd be capable of doing well because of my interests, or indulgences." Here a smile. "I *have* read a lot and once I did some writing, none of it published, but . . ."

I went on, endlessly on, till he stopped me. They had a lot of excellent fiction on their spring list. In truth, how-

ever, fiction didn't make money. Texts are the thing. Education is the market now. Trade nonfiction generally outsells
fiction. I knew that, didn't I?

"Yes. Of course."

"We don't have to approve of it. But we supply, and they
buy."

Douglas Flannery liked a slogan.

He brought the forms up a bit late, dropped them uncertainly between us on the desk. In leaning forward I un-
crossed a leg. In doing so I kicked forward, caught the sharp
underside of his desk with my shin. Hard enough for him to
hear it. Pain, wambling pain. I bent forward, dropping my
purse to pick it up and rub my hurt. Merciful blood, tip
back into my mad head. It did. But Douglas was at my side.

"I kicked the damn desk," I blurted, tearing slightly.

"I'm sorry." He bent down and patted my shoulder; his
face swollen and porous at that range. A fevered breath.

"I'm all right now." But there was a bloodless white in-
dention visible through the stocking and a runner beginning.
I rubbed the dent with my finger tips. We looked at it.

I said: "I'm fine, Mr. Flannery. As fine as a clumsy idiot
can be. Never safe. Anyone who could kick a desk is never
quite safe." I capped that with a neat giggle.

He resumed his seat and staunching procedures after I
insisted. And I took the application forms.

He began a paternal, proud discussion of editorial duties.
It took time. I smiled, frowned, yessed and noed, shook my
head in wonder when he discussed the miracle of co-opera-
tion, each of my reactions an amplified repeat of what I
thought he felt. And again I got a kind of breezy feeling. On
my way.

Then he brought down trouble: "Now, Nina, and I hope

you don't mind my calling you Nina, I've told you all you need to know about us. You tell us about you. Who is Nina Ward?"

"Oh, ho, ho," I began. And I will go no further now. It is not a remarkable past. I can't recall what I said anyway. I began with a sentence that seemed unendable. I finished off in little phrases interspersed with a variety of tics and scratches. The main theme established itself quickly. I went to a Methodist teachers' college, the name of which I always have to repeat. And I had never worked except once, as a model, in a Los Angeles department store, when our boys were coming home from the war. (Let me be fair to myself; I worked illegally; I was underage.)

Douglas, during this phase of the interview, brought out two or three pharmaceutical bottles from his desk and applied their contents liberally. He was not perfect, not by any means. He used nose drops as well. Right there, without a nod.

But he had reason for relaxing. Clearly the tenor of the interview had changed.

"In a year or two," he said, head back, sniffing, "your experience—"

"Lack of it—"

"—won't make a bit of difference." He sniffed again. "We want workers, not illustrious undergraduates. I hope I don't offend you when I say that your maturity can be an asset. You must know that young women, in the hardened mind of the businessman, are considered a dubious risk. We train them and they go forth and give birth. Not that we would have it any other way, but there is a considerable investment in our training program.

"But you'll understand that a certain specialization is

usually preferred. You can see that, Nina, I imagine?"

"Yes. I'm sorry I'm not able to—" I put the forms down again.

"Oh, don't get the impression I'm turning you away. Not at all. We can't rely entirely on playing it safe. We take chances with our people. Please, please keep the papers."

So I retrieved them, and made as if to go when, adjusting his shirt sleeves, Mr. Flannery glanced at his watch.

"Wait. Before you go, we have something else to cover. Haven't we?"

"Yes?"

"The money. Salary. We haven't mentioned it yet."

"I'd forgotten it." And I had. That's one reason why I've written this.

"I won't try now to describe the profit-sharing system we are thinking of inaugurating when we change locations."

"You're leaving this lovely old building?"

"It's completely inadequate. A ruin. We aren't even air-conditioned. To get back to cash, and about this I'm not absolutely certain, because the raises come pretty frequently, I believe you would draw five hundred and some—say, fifty—a month. Then an automatic five-dollar raise, per week, of course, after six months.

"Five hundred dollars." I repeated it. Twice. Then, figuring quickly, I said: "About a hundred and thirty per week?"

"Maybe more. Some. If we start that plan you'll be getting a raise daily."

"Five hundred fifty." In some odd way, I took strength here. "What does a regular editor make?" I inquired.

I've forgotten his reply.

"What do you make?" I went on, seriously.

"Well, of course, I have a certain . . ." He stopped. "I take it you require more?"

"No. Oh, no. Not at all." I waved the application forms. "I just wondered about the future."

"The future with us is good."

So ended the interview. I stood up and said good-bye without shaking hands, but beaming thankfulness, a radiant gratitude. Then an idiotic idea came to me. I was on my way out. I stopped.

"Mr. Flannery, would you let me take you to lunch. I've taken up so much of your time I feel I should . . ."

He shook his head. "Thank you, no." He went back to his desk and took from it a paper bag. "Economizing," he said. "The wife and I are touring Europe next summer."

V

I took a cab back. Arnold Schurman. I remember their names because I left a bag in a cab once. I threw the forms out on Twelfth Street.

I paused outside near the garbage cans, planning my entry, which would include a rush to the bathroom, a shower, laughter all the while, and a disconnected account of what had happened, shouted over the roar of water.

Roi started barking as soon as I entered. I interpret his barks. At the door he jumped on me, tongue lolling into the suds that clung to his whiskers and collapsed topknot. He was covered with gray soap bubbles and he was dripping. The rug was wet, and when he shook himself he flung mud on my clothes, the door, walls, this typewriter.

Myra walked out of the bathroom crying; she wore my shorts and my halter, and she was filthy.

"For God's *sake*," I think I said. "What have you done?"

"I was trying to help. I tried to bathe him."

"Get some towels and dry him."

"He *snaps* at me. He let me put the shampoo on, but now he snaps at me."

"Idiot! Call the pet service. I'll get some towels."

Here I took command, displaying considerable hauteur. Marching into the bathroom, I drew on a robe. I took soiled towels from the hamper. I carried a chair out to the laundry area. When Roi came and placed his chin on my knee, I wiped first around his eyes, where he was most sensitive. He tried a few wags but gave in quickly to the discomfort. He shivered, and keened deep in his throat.

Myra came out to us. "They can't pick him up for three hours. That's the earliest. We'll have to go in a cab. Let's wrap him up and call a cab. I'll pay, Nina. For everything."

"No. It's chilly out. And no one will take him in a cab. He'll get it filthy. He looks awful and he smells. I'll have to bathe him myself."

"I'm terribly sorry. I'll get your furniture cleaned. Nothing's really hurt. It's mostly water and soap. And filth. If you took better care of that damned dog, you'd—"

So I told her to leave. I said:

"While I'm in there, you get your things ready and go. Be gone when I come out."

"What?" She was incredulous, rightfully so. "For God's sake, you *can't* mean it!"

"I mean it. Leave. Get the hell out."

"But I smell of dog. I'm filthy. *Damn* it, Nina, you . . ."

She complained too forcefully. Roi, my guardian, symbol, and sole friend, growled.

She rushed off. And for three or four minutes, while I

moved her things out of the bathroom cabinet—wrapped her toothbrush in toilet tissue, did the same with a brush and comb—I felt strong. I put soap and a hand towel out so she could wash at the kitchen sink. But I think the articles arranged on a chair outside the bathroom door changed all that. It reminded me of sending Sara off to school. There's a difference between what I feel while getting her ready and what follows, when she's gone.

Myra sobbed mightily in the next room. Her suitcase snapped once, and I heard, in its place, a suicide weapon being cocked. But then Roi sneezed at the appropriate moment.

So I undressed and drew on my shower cap, started the water from outside the curtain, adjusting. The stall is new, metal-sided, loud. It got steamy with the door closed. Roi lay down on the floor, nose pressed to the crack under the door. I stepped into the shower; leaning out, water pelting my back, I called him.

He looked up, uncertain.

I called again.

Not at his ease, not eagerly, he came.

It was a hard job cleaning him, and a harder one getting him dry, but I did well. We spent a pleasant afternoon in the kitchen, all alone, with the oven on and the oven door open. Roi basked in the heat while I brushed my hair over the table, over the *Times*, opened to another section—sports, I believe.

I was—am now—doing what I do the best. I was thankful; in a way, I suppose, happy. And Roi didn't get sick, hasn't been sick since, for which I thank God.

THE RITE OF LATIN HIPS

The Monster Awaits

The baby's initial cooing awakened him. So long as he lay
perfectly still, the cooing was sweet, the world gentle. But
he rolled over and God reached down out of heaven with a
pair of judgmatic pincers and drew him upright, to meet his
deeds. The pincers' jaws bit into his skull just above his
eyes and, on the left side, just above his ears and, at the
rear, low down, where the spine joined. He came directly
up, pulling the single sheet (it was summer then) off his
naked wife. For one moment the pain was so intense that
tears came to his eyes. He moaned.

The baby in the crib in their room began to cry.

From the adjacent bedroom the sound of wild plunging
that signaled the arrival at consciousness of his other daughter.

The Size of Trouble

His hangover and the demands of the children were like

two celestial bodies on a collision course, hurtling toward each other at the speed of light. He was a kite in space, borne by the strenuous current of his guilt into the paths of these onrushing bodies. The morning would kill him.

"Daddeeee. Bring me milk-koooooo." His eldest daughter, Kate.

Molly, the baby, ceased to cry; she screamed.

"All *right*," he said.

He scooped the baby from her crib, held her close to him. She was hot; her head smelled sour. He soothed her with soft words and gentle patting. She quieted down quickly enough.

Brief Recollection of Pleasure

His sleeping wife rolled over. She had her pearls on, and one pearl earring. Lipstick. Her breasts leaned outward, the nipples pointed up and away. One, the left one, was trained on him, a sightless mauve eye. Her body seemed immense in the bad light. Pale, it blended with the shadows of tangled sheets; hair, cupped navel, dark nails were landmarks enough, but the skin seemed to sweep outward from her, continue to the edge of the bed, square off, drop away.

A broad field he'd conquered, drunkenly, a few hours earlier. A rough male mounting, volleys and thrusts, and orgasm a final neural broadside. She had fallen asleep in an instant. The memory of sex, like muscle ache after athletics, made him feel strong, young.

"Daddeeee. Milk-koooo." Kate's daily beg, half whimper, made him smile. The baby pressed her mouth to his shoulder and began to gum him. Nude still, he went off to the kitchen. With each step, each time his heels struck the floor, his brain vibrated ominously; and, yes, the taste of the monster's food was in his mouth. Still, he could have felt worse.

Duties, Services

He ran the hot-water tap and started a burner. He got Molly's formula from the fridge, a pan from the cupboard. Water—two inches of the hottest—into the pan; bottle in that. He took Kate's bottle out of the fridge and carried it back down the hallway.

She was singing, and he stood, Molly sucking the shoulder, milk in hand, outside her door.

"Katie had a lit tul lamp
Lit tul lamp
Katie had a lit tul lamp
Lit tul lamp"

Lines left out, same self-centered alterations of text, but she was right on key. At less than two and a half, she had an ear. Both were pretty children, but that could change.

For no apparent reason, he began to worry about nausea.

He entered Kate's room. She sat in the center of her large crib, legs folded beneath her, hands on knees, chanting. Her hair was tangled. A small green bow had slipped down one hank almost to the end. The father saw it as a butterfly, stopped there for a moment, before continuing its flickering way through the world.

"Here's your milk. Now you drink it and be quiet."

First Shock

"That your tail?" she asked, staring at his organs of reproduction.

He dropped the bottle beside her and left the room, shamed. He had forgotten; why had he forgotten?

First Denial

Clad now in khaki walking shorts, he fed the baby in the bedroom, seated on the edge of his bed. He had taken two aspirins with his orange juice. The taste of the juice had immediately given way to the taste of corruption. His tongue felt cool and greasy. He held his head averted to keep from breathing the miasma on the innocent infant.

He was surprised to find his wife awake. She lay completely still, her eyes wide open.

"Hi," he said.

She blinked.

"How're you feeling? I thought I'd let you sleep a little longer." He was his cheery, generous self, in tone and action.

She continued to stare at the ceiling.

"I don't feel so bad," he said. "Considering that I put quite a bit away. A lot, in fact. But all that swimming and dancing works it off. Athletic parties, they are."

Molly pulled away from the bottle and screeched. He put her over his shoulder and rubbed her back. She squirmed and whimpered. He felt a ball of gas, like something solid, detach itself from the hard little stomach and shoot upward. She burped powerfully, her head recoiling on the flimsy neck. He laughed at the noise. (In fact, he forced himself to laugh at the noise.)

His wife turned to look at the child, the same blank expression on her face. She turned to the ceiling again. Was it fatigue kept her distant?

"What's wrong? You know you forgot to wash? You didn't even take off your pearls, and you've lost an earring. Probably knocked off when I—"

"No."

Something in her tone—dispassion and cold contempt—riled his viscera.

"No, what?"

He brought Molly down to his lap again and returned the bottle to her mouth. She smiled around the rubber nipple. Great little face, monkey bright and loving. And eyes. Eyes vulnerably blue, as if they had been colored with a crayon, as if a careless touch would knock free flecks of color.

First Odious Revelation

"You took the earring off, threw it in the swimming pool, and challenged everyone to dive for it. No one did but you, and you couldn't find it."

He had not forgotten that; because he had never recorded it.

"It *was* a stupid trick. I'm sorry. Another dumb, drunken, show-offy—"

She turned over and pulled the pillow around her ears.

"I'm going right over and dive for it this morning," he announced.

The pillow imperfectly blocked sound. She said: "Bob and Barbara are coming over here this morning."

He almost cursed: Guests? Why, for God's sake? But experience with evil had taught him to proceed with caution.

"What time? Did we set a time? I've forgotten. Maybe I could pick them up."

"I don't know. We're leaving early, since we are going

to Newport Beach. You and he are going to buy a boat, you remember. Try a little charter fishing. Ten grand should start you off nicely. I wonder if you had pearl fishing in mind when you threw my earring away."

Attempt at Minimization

He laughed. The whole idea struck him as impossible and comic. He had work to do that afternoon, a series of summer-school lectures to prepare. He got seasick on any craft smaller than the *Queen Mary*. He could raise perhaps a thousand dollars.

"Bob thought it was funny too. Until you got mad and started acting like you were being insulted. And making cracks about people with money."

"I'll call and apologize. And tell them to stay away."

"Fine with me."

He burped the baby again, went in to see Kate, to find out why she was so quiet, he said. He expected to find her asleep. She was still sitting up; she held the bottle up, tilted, at the angle of a herald's horn.

What Kate Heralded

He was worried, suddenly. Bob was his department head. His wife probably had more to reveal. His stomach began to squirm inside him. (The monster was awake now.) The brain vibrations continued whether he walked or not.

His Defense

"You lie down in bed and drink that milk like a big girl," he ordered.

It was nonsense, and the child recognized it as such. She didn't remove the bottle, didn't speak. She just shook her head.

Back with Molly to the bedroom.

Second Odious Revelation

"While you're calling, you might give Miss Saltonstall a ring. I believe you bit her ear. While dancing. While ten or twelve of your colleagues and superiors were getting knocked around by your romantic lurches. You've developed some wonderful new spins, my dear. And Latin hips. Those ludicrous Latin hips."

Monster in Command

He placed the baby and her bottle in the bed with his wife and assumed the classic attitude of self-loathing: seated at edge of bed, hunched over, head clasped between hands, palms over ears.

Miss Saltonstall shared his office and book space. She was attractive, young. He had looked at her and wondered. But he found faults: hirsute arms, a cloud of dizzying perfume that hid rather than enticed, hair cut so close it reminded him of an Army helmet liner.

Besides, he was genuinely uxorious, a family man, most of the time. And now he had to face her in the morning (it was Sunday), and how would he do that? As a lover with his hat in the ring? Or as a reformed drunk, morose and humble, his woeful flagellant's eyes avoiding hers, avoiding error? Bit her ear, for the love of God! Had he drawn blood; did everyone know? Had they heard her scream out?

He remembered nothing. He swore aloud. His apology

followed. He pleaded the occasional monster. He reminded her that its visits were infrequent, of short duration.

She had placed the baby between herself and the wall. She was facing away, and very silent.

Swim! Strike Out! Where There's a Sea, There's a Reef!

The sheet's hem crossed her hips at the top of the arch. Her skin had deepened in hue now, as a lager-colored light filtered in through drawn blinds. Shadows curved on her back and upper buttocks. Strong, sweet flesh, grand to the touch. Desire took him, a sober need but blood brother of last night's rapacity. He leaned over, at the expense of what little physical comfort he enjoyed, and drew the sheet farther down.

She drew it up. "I hate you," she said.

Mirror on Despair

Kate called out as he was rushing to the bathroom. (He wanted to see himself again, to ascertain who he was this morning.) The cry meant that she had sloughed off torpor. She was ready for the world, demanded her release. Her freedom meant an end to his privacy. So he went on.

Before the mirror the headache intensified. All other pains gave way to a clapper throb that boomed through him, hollowed him out and rang him like a bell. Nausea groped its way into possibility. Fight it! He breathed deeply, threw tap water on his face and chest. He peered through hopeless eyes at hopeless eyes. No savage stared back at him. A sea of red wash isolated his old, hardened irises.

Miss Saltonstall's exuberant reek drifted to mind. He re-

called stiff shoulders and a look of disguised terror as, he
supposed, they danced. She had grinned and he had spun
her out. Had his hand slipped? Had she bumped someone?
Ev Walker, in Fine Arts? Had glass shattered?

Memory Plays a Hand

A month before, he had proposed to the wife of a mathematics instructor that they elope to Cuba. "Exile among the
purposeful and doomed," he had repeated many times, with
what his wife called a "noble" expression on his face.

Two months before that, at Bob's and Barbara's, he had
scraped his forehead on the bottom of their swimming pool
during some exhibition diving. For the rest of the evening,
until the dried gore ran the other guests off, he had sat
about with the gash uncovered and untreated. His monster
had, in that instance, assumed a British accent, made crisp
references to "other people, secret people, here to snap our
spines."

He was regarded as funny when drunk, a "wild" dancer, a
good party man, by a diminishing few.

The Real Trouble

If he began those evenings as Dionysus, if the wives of
teachers and Miss Saltonstall and his wife were blurred into
a crew of poolside Bacchae, somewhere during the celebra-
tions, a transformation took place. Gothic horrors were all
that remained in the morning. He had every reason to doubt
that he performed in the rituals. Memory failed him. What
he knew was discovered through his wife. And he found her
hard to believe.

Yes, there was something that possessed him. For he had faith in himself, as father, husband, lover.

It was in the latter role alone that the gap between him and the monster was bridged. He and the incubus united to fall upon his helpless wife. The three fell asleep. In the morning he awoke, an indistinct recollection of pleasure the one balm for his violated senses. And he knew that the loving itself was too fierce, too mad, to please his partner.

The Rules of Love

Kate passed a very dirty fingernail between her front teeth. She waited for her father, leaning over the edge of the crib.

"Take your finger out of your mouth," he said.

Her eyes were gray, wide open, empty as outthrust beggars' palms. An hour after she was born he had held her in his arms; even when she was too small to love, he had made preposterous pledges to himself concerning her protection. Now he felt he could not perform the simplest duties to her. If he had been given a knife and led into a chamber where she lay, her sweet skin folded back over a diseased heart, he would not have felt more useless.

"What do you want?"

"I want some vitamins. I want down."

To insure against forgetting the vitamins, he administered them before lifting her over the rail. He went to the fridge, got vitamins, went to the cupboard, got teaspoon. Back in the bedroom he poured out a teaspoonful of a black liquid that smelled, faintly, like Miss Saltonstall's perfume.

Kate scowled but took it.

He capped the bottle and lifted her up.

"Give Daddy a good-morning squeeze?" She began her

enviably easy ritual. As always, on such mornings, he felt he would one day ruin her life, because of his drinking.

"Yes," he answered, when she was already straining, thin arms no tighter than a necktie around his neck. Oh, she was weak. So was Molly. And his wife was weakening.

He answered his daughter's squeeze with such a sudden, frenzied rush of love and fear that she cried out.

"You squeeze me too much."

And he apologized to her.

Second Denial

His wife called him while he was taking Kate to the bathroom. Molly needed two ounces more. She was starving.

"It's those damned baby sitters. They refuse to give a kid a late bottle."

"They aren't so bad. The children are safe with them."

A Voice from the Air

While the supplement heated, he took Kate to the bathroom and removed the sour, coiled diapers. (She wore a doubled diaper at night.) He covered her loins with talc and got clean panties for her and clean shorts. Dressed alike, they returned to the kitchen, where he gave her orange juice and asked her to sing. She refused, asked that the radio be turned on. He turned it on. A minister of the gospel, a woman with a hoarse, Midwestern voice, unleashed her piety on the innocent and unaccepting alike.

"Loving God is not loving ourselves. The Bible bids us love, but does not tell us to direct our love inward, upon a vain and insignificant being. Outward, then; outward upon God's meek and miserable, upon the misguided, the mistaken; there, *there*, is where we find those who hunger for love, cry out for the reach of—"

He shut it off.

"That lady not singing?"

"No."

The formula was too hot. He had to cool it off, tilting the bottle in a pan and letting cold water from the tap run over its surface. He put his daughter in her high chair, bibbed her, and gave her cereal, a new brand with dehydrated fruit in corn flakes. Shriveled bits of strawberry tumbled from the box. He poured milk over all, stood for a moment, to make certain she did not pick out the fruit alone. The faint odor of the strawberries at once brought back Miss Saltonstall and sickened him. He took the formula and walked out.

Third Denial

The baby and her mother were in the same positions but the sheet had shifted, slipped. The stronger light revealed the dimpled abundance of her milky butt. A soothing proprietary power stole over him as he handed her the bottle. She half turned to take it; a breast reared up. The shaded armpit and sweep of bosom lay like good land before his ambitious eye. He laid his hand in the saddle of her hip, bent over and pressed his lips to the hillock above the hand. She shuddered.

"Quit."

"At least we—I—do make love when I'm drunk. It may be a little on the side of rape, but—"

"No," his wife said, pulling up the sheet and giving Molly the bottle.

"Of course we do."

"Not last night, we didn't. I wouldn't let you."

"The *hell*. I remember that. It may be a little hazy . . ."
He waited, scared.

"Where were we?"

"Right here," he said. He turned; their clothes were
thrown in a chair. Only the clothes of lovers could be so
intermingled. "There are our clothes."

"Where did you first kiss me?"

"Well . . . I . . . What difference does it make?"

"Did we make love on the bed, in the living room, on
the floor, in the bathroom? Where? *Where?*"

"Don't yell, the baby's eating."

"Where?"

"Here. In the bed."

She shook her head. "No."

"I remember. Distinctly." But he didn't. And he was
beginning to feel very bad.

"If you remember that, you remember driving home.
Going for two miles without the lights, to test your night
vision. And then trying the cornering ability of the car. You
wouldn't let me drive. When I asked you, you laughed. And
when I begged you to stop, you drove faster. Do you remember? Now? Is it still distinct?"

"No," he said. The beast inside seemed to be enjoying
himself now. He was dancing a jig in his stomach.

"I wouldn't have anything to do with a stinking drunken
pig. I'm not your Miss Saltonstall."

Confrontation

His awareness of general betrayal set up a complementary
queasiness. His viscera seemed to flutter into a huge, un-

healthy life. He was reminded of great, heavy-bodied birds, their clumsy exertions in getting air-borne.

Yes, he knew the feeling.

Exorcism

He returned to the bathroom, grabbed the edges of the two soaking diapers, and began to rinse them out with a haste born of emergency. Water sloshed over the thick rim of the basin, hit his feet, the floor. He withdrew the diapers and wrung them out. He dropped them at the side of the toilet. He went to the basin and washed his hands with a physician's thoroughness. He did not look at the face in the mirror now, the glow of cold sweat on putty cheeks and brow.

"Daddeee. My cereal fall on the floor."

He dried his hands carefully on the towel. Kate's call meant that she was finished eating and would pour the remainder on the kitchen floor if he did not come and take her out of the high chair. He could not help her now. He could not call out.

"Daddeee. My cereal fall on the floor."

He heard it slosh down, the plastic bowl bump and bounce, then roll.

"She spilled it, you know," his wife said.

He knew, but he was now kneeling slowly before the toilet, lowering himself to his knees, maintaining his balance with soap-scented hands over, but not touching, the septic porcelain. His kneecaps touched the wet tile. The odor of urine dizzied him. (The idea of washing it away was canceled by the idea of deserved suffering.)

He inserted two clean fingers of his right hand into his

mouth, touched the soft palate. His gorge rose; he waited, reached again.

A Conclusion without an End

Up it came. A convulsive push that bent him forward; he vomited a weak arch of orange liquid, in quantity slight. He coughed to clear a bitter residue from his gullet. He spat again, stared at the pool before him.

Nothing. A foul slime. The monster had escaped or remained within. A film on the water in which no face appeared, no wicked symbol formed for him to ponder. Not enough. He shoved the hand back down.

"Are you sick?" his wife called.

"Daddeee, where are you?" Kate called.

He wiggled his fingers, waited for an answer.

KITCHEN INTERLUDE

Bernard and Simone Wein lived with their young son, Karl, in four boxy little rooms on the fourth floor. The rooms were situated around two sides of an air shaft. In winter foul weather got into the shaft and swirled about on currents of wind. Drops of rain and snowflakes could be seen whirling about in a horizontal spin or making vertical dashes from the leaden sky that ejected them. The kitchen window of the Weins' apartment overlooked the shaft; the frame of the lower pane was painted fast, stuck at an angle, so that whatever storm raged outside found hissing entrance into the room.

During the three days that Sandra Coffman was on this earth, she was located in the center of the kitchen table, back to the glass. It was winter then—a winter in the early sixties—and she took the brunt of rain and wind on the back of her neck.

Sandra—who wanted so to be called Sandy, and never was —appeared early one weekday morning. Karl awakened, shouted for his father from the crib. Bernard, who slept naked in all seasons, lay wrapped around his warm wife like a snake in a tree. He dropped away, prompted by the boy's cries, climbed from the bed, and trotted the short hallway to the kitchen.

He snapped on the light. He went first to the stove, where a bottle of milk had been placed on the porcelain directly over the griddle pilot, so it would not be freezing. Bottle in hand, he turned to the table, where there were a hand of overripe bananas, a bottle of candy-flavored vitamin pills, and Sandra.

She had already seen him. She had her eyes slammed shut.

Bernard, on seeing her, dropped the bottle, rushed across, grabbed Sandra by the hair with one hand, and with the other tried to force open the window. The window would not move, but his intention was clear. He was going to throw her out, without question.

Sandra gasped. Bernard heaved, and the bottle of tablets fell; pills rolled everywhere, and the bananas rose on finger tips and walked off the edge of the table.

Sandra began to scream. (She seemed to have all the vocal apparatus necessary for screaming, singing, and ordinary conversation, and she could feel pain.)

Simone Wein heard the noise and her husband's swearing, and she rushed in.

"What is it?" she said, in French.

"Not—goddamnit—mine!" Bernard spoke English with an accent.

"Take it out."

"It won't go."

Sandra, hearing a woman's voice, said: "Take him away. Make him dress. Please." Her eyes were still closed. Tears leaked from beneath the lids.

When she spoke, Bernard gave another tug to her hair. Simone was the calm one. She told him in French that he would be sick if he did not dress. He had his work. Go and put on some warm clothes.

"Speak English!" Sandra shouted. "Please. And make him leave."

Then Karl came in. The bottle and the candy-flavored tablets were pacifiers which permitted the parents to remain in bed a few minutes longer each morning. He could easily climb from his crib. Karl was a handsome boy, not quite three, already bilingual.

"Where is the leg?" he asked, after walking boldly up to the table, squatting to peer beneath it, then circling to the sides.

There was more than a leg missing.

Sandra Coffman was a handsome head and neck, a pretty girl. She had ice-blue eyes, large and wondrous; she had beautiful American teeth and full lips; her nose, with its mild Celtic tilt, robbed her of beauty but insured against the inertness perfection sometimes imposes; and the pallor of her face, implying fragility, saved her from being cute. She was advertising-pretty perhaps, but very much that.

Her attractiveness was startling, but it offered no protection. She was an unarmed invader, and Bernard, dressing, considered only this. When he returned he went to the pantry for a kitchen knife and spatula. He attempted to insert both blades between neck and tabletop, but he chose unsharpened utensils, so he was not willing to draw blood. Sandra adhered, shouted that she was being pinched, and again screamed.

"Shut up!" Bernard said. He clamped his hand over her mouth. She bit him, sent him hopping around, crushing vitamins underfoot.

Simone led her injured husband and amazed son into another room.

In half an hour a startling silence had settled over the apartment. The Wein family ate dry cereal in their living room. Bernard repeatedly said: "We will have business as usual."

And Simone nodded, rather sadly. Business as usual meant that she and Karl played soundless games in the kitchen during the winter. In the summer they were sent from the house. Bernard was writing his thesis in the bedroom, and he had to have at least two walls separating him from all other living creatures to facilitate concentration. With Sandra occupying the table, Simone and Karl would have to go out into the storm.

"You will go out, get a bus, ride to Union Square, find a cafeteria, and purchase coffee for yourself, hot chocolate for the boy. Don't empty your cups, or they will take them away and you will have to buy more."

Bernard was very firm, his plan was polished, yet he was obviously upset. He was pacing about, biting the inside of his lip. There was a human head on his table. What the hell? A human head, alive. Why?

I am condensing Bernard's biography because he would never divulge anything about himself unless begged. I have also of necessity invented some things, for I would not beg. He was born in Vienna, outside the Ring, twenty-eight years before this narrative begins. His father owned some kind of business, a shop, I should think, and when the Nazis came, he was able to trade the business for safe passage out of the country for himself and his family.

They went to Paris, Amsterdam, and London. Bernard lived as a cousin with a Dutch family during most of the war, and if he paid any country a modicum of patriotic respect, Holland was the recipient. His father was in hiding. Bernard never knew him well. He remembered a rough hand, smelling of gasoline, and awakening from his sleep when it rested lightly on his forehead. His father's health was ruined by the time the war ended. Shortly after Berlin fell, the Weins sailed for South America, and Mr. Wein died aboard ship. His kidneys failed him. He was buried at sea.

His mother took a factory job in Buenos Aires in order to save money to send her one son back to Europe. He left first; she was to follow. He returned to the family that had sheltered him during the occupation, and word of his mother's death reached him some months later. A letter, written in German and signed by the translator, Herr O. Bilder, requested that money be sent immediately to cover the unpaid rent of her hotel room. Legal action was threatened. The police, in going through the effects of the deceased, had found nothing of value, nothing to compensate for the funeral expenses.

They were high because the burial could not take place in Catholic earth due to the circumstances of the death.

Bernard was always a brilliant student, as you would expect. Scholarship had pulled him through his crises. When nations went mad and war was outside the window, as current and broadcast as the air itself, Bernard read, learned languages, thought. When they lowered his father's coffin into the ocean, he was reading a book on Napoleon, and he knew a good deal more about the Emperor than he ever would about his Max Wein. Ideas and the imprint of famous men survived. If he continued to read and study, he would stuff his head with all that was durable and therefore truly alive.

He came to America because scholars were paid well to work.

But he never trusted his wife, or his handsome, bottle-sucking son, or himself to go on living for another five minutes. They were all perishable. His thesis was in no danger of kidney infection, wouldn't develop suicidal tendencies. And as it was part of him, it represented a sort of immunity. Or it would when he was finished.

So, on that first morning, when Sandra Coffman occupied the kitchen, Bernard went in and sat down at his desk. He didn't believe he would be able to work; but he would languish at the altar, honor the dogma. Sandra was quiet. (She was asleep.) On his desk were some note cards and an ancient portable typewriter. He picked up a note card. On it was written an English sentence so Germanic in formation it might have been a literal translation. (His sentences are reminiscent of an aerial photograph of a train wreck.)

I cannot begin to discuss the subject of his thesis. Pages of graphs and statistical breakdowns make me faint, to tell the truth. It had to do with a definition of class for a class-less society. In a few footnotes he attacked the methods of conclusions of honored scholars in his field, and in the warmth of his dismissals he did at least give way to envy, anger, smugness. In the body of his work the train-wreck sentences crashed into one another, but the freight was apparently undisturbed. There were already publishers from university presses after it. That pleased him.

So he read the one note card, saw a place where he could

insert another subordinate clause, plugged it in, then realized how this clause would effect the sentences that were to follow.

In a moment or two he was hard at work. He got in a good hour.

"Mr. Way-ane," Sandra called. She then yawned audibly. "Mr. Way-ane, if-you-don't-answer-I'll scree-eam." She sang it, as if she were trying to make her threats pleasant.

Bernard thrust his papers from him, rose. He went into the kitchen.

Already she had entered her decline, though it was as yet scarcely noticeable. The window behind her squirted foul weather onto the back of her head and a swatch of pale neck. Her hairdo began to wilt, slightly.

"What do you want here?" Bernard said, affecting bored curiosity.

"I'm sorry to bother you, but I have a couple of little favors to ask. I think there is garlic on the table, and I'm allergic to garlic. My nose is tickly." She quivered it, rabbit-like, to demonstrate. "Also it's cold and wet here, with the window open."

"I will not wipe your *nose!*"

"No, no. I only wondered if you would just wipe up the table around me a tiny bit. And close the window. Please."

He would do nothing.

"Mr. Wayne, let's be adult. There's no reason why we can't get along. I don't know why I'm here. I certainly don't want to *be* here. But I can't move and you can't move me."

"I could take the table apart. I could kill you."

"If I'm the kind of person who dies, I might still come back. Maybe in another place. Where you work, or your bedroom, or . . . or . . ."

"Only Karl's room and the bath are left. Perhaps you would reappear in the bathroom." Bernard seemed to enjoy that idea.

Sandra did not. "That *couldn't* be."

She was right.

"Listen, let's be friends." She smiled. "You call me Sandy and I'll call you . . . ah . . . Bernie."

"And your surname? What is that?"

"Coffman."

It was at this point that Bernard found similarity between her surname and Franz Kafka's. "Kafka becomes Coffman? Is *that* it? Some simplistic plagiarist has attempted, without success, to shock me with a ridiculous . . ." This sentence would have been endless had Sandra not interrupted Bernard with a meek—and almost soundless—sneeze. It was extremely human, delightfully mortal.

Bernard said: "You are getting a cold. A *head* cold." He began to laugh. "What could be worse for you?"

Ho ho ho.

He left, spinning on his heel. He went into the living room, sprawled on the couch, and began a catalogue of possible explanations for Sandra's presence. He was thorough, and not one to reveal his method or conclusion until he had worried it through. He was still caught up in the analytical process at noon, when his wife and son returned.

That afternoon, when Karl was sleeping and Simone and Bernard were lying in bed, intertwined against the cold but not in the entangled attitude of lovers (only the kitchen could be kept warm in the afternoons, when the oven was lighted, and the oven door dropped open like the jaw of a benign dragon), Sandra Coffman sang a song. Perhaps never

in the history of popular music was a simple lyric treated
with such hermeneutical care. I quote it in full:

Bitter my heart
Since you've gone.
Broken my dreams
With each dawn.

Why did you leave
Me alone?
Where are the joys
We have known?

These lonely hours
Like faded flowers,
Letters of love,
All fade about me—
Because you doubt me.
Bring back my love.

Why are you staying
Away?
Bring back the sun to
    my day.
Then I will cry no more.
Bitter my heart.

It was several minutes of silence before Bernard pronounced "Bitter My Heart" as shit, in French. Simone sadly
agreed.

"But it is strange that she sings," she added.

"Too goddamn strange," Bernard said, and he jumped
from the bed. He was dressed, lacking only shoes and socks.
He walked briskly into the kitchen.

"I have seen the detached heads of your women on television! Blonde, shallow, sexless creatures, constantly in a panic of false desire, dehumanized by a culture which—"

Sandra shook her head (herself) solemnly, with nothing that even resembled fear or abashment evident in her features. Bernard ceased talking.

"I was singing because I was bored. If someone around here would just *talk* to me a little bit—I mean, *that's* what I want. I want company."

Bernard obscenely dismissed the idea of talking to her. Then: "Do you suppose I can feel sorrow for you? Are we to find you somehow sad? I reserve my pity for Man. And you do not qualify."

Later that evening Sandra took advantage of Simone's dinner preparations to engage her in conversation. It was largely the girl's monologue, for Simone scarcely listened. Strange how a head alone had assimilated those qualities that would require, one would think, the fully developed and functioning human body. For example, Sandra's touching desires for a home of her own, a husband (yes!), a modern kitchen.

"Not," she said, "that there is anything wrong with yours. It's very compact. Things are handy."

Simone was preparing some sauce or other. She appeared not to be listening. Her unresponsiveness drove Sandra on.

"Most of all," she said, quite forcefully, "I want a child. My *own* child. I think of having a little daughter, a tiny little baby with—"

"And how would you carry this child? How would you deliver it? Perhaps you could cough it, as your name suggests."

Bernard, just outside the door, listening for clues, pondering Sandra's every word, was delighted by his wife. Punning in her second language, in a time of stress, with a detached head on her table. What a woman!

Not much sleep for Bernard that night, though Simone and Karl were not so disrupted. They assumed, prematurely, that the male adult head-of-house was perfectly capable of ushering them both through any crisis. Bernard listened to the rustling sounds of Sandra's respiration. She suffered two or three fits of sneezing. Two or three times she moaned softly.

"Ohhh. I'm sooo cooold."

Bernard Wein didn't pity her. He too was cold; so, probably, was his son. Bernard's mind did not provide the insular warmth for his sleeping family, and it was at the boundaries of his immediate family that all sympathy stopped.

He lay, wide awake, remarking her Germanic name, her inane statements, her ingenuousness, her helplessness, her sexless femininity. All these provided tempting themes for hypotheses. But she—Sandra, the blonde—could not be significant; Bernard could scarcely try her in the test of some extended speculation.

He slept fitfully; he awoke when he dreamed he heard her calling, and he did hear the footsteps of his son beat down the hall. Karl, up early, called for his bottle.

Sandra asked him for a tissue. The child fetched one, climbed on the table, and held it before her nose.

"Blow," he said.

Bernard charged in, wearing trousers, slapped Karl's hands, forced the boy to wash them, then washed his own. He might have slapped Sandra, but he recalled a theory, considered and rejected during the night.

"You are here to arouse doubt of my humane feelings in

the mind of my son," he said. "Let me tell you something: If he became so frightened of me, so disappointed, so precociously decent that he took his things and left my house, promising to leave forever, and disappeared into the cold streets of this charming New World metropolis, I would let him go. *Let him go!* Do you understand? To pity something like you is to be as stupid as you are. I will *not* permit a simple mind to develop in my home!"

He left the room.

But he gave up work that morning, spent hours with Karl, giving the poor child difficult language exercises in French and, when the boy became tired, in Dutch. In the afternoon the three of them had a luncheon at the small, excellent delicatessen on the corner of Tenth Street and Second Avenue and attended the matinee at an inexpensive neighborhood movie house frequented by elderly people and the more solvent or tired of neighborhood derelicts.

When, after dark, they returned to their apartment, all three walked to the kitchen, paused on the threshold and listened. Sandra hissed brokenly. Karl, the first into the room, said: "She is not the same."

The dampness spitting through the window had collected in her hair, soaked it through, so it pressed limply against the back of her skull. Yet the sides and the bangs were dry. Her face was blotchy, probably feverish. When she opened her eyes, the pupils seemed to stare out of a bed of coals.

She sniffed, rather heroically, and smiled.

"Back so soon? How was the film, Karl? Sit near your Aunt Sandy and tell her—"

Simone took her son's hand and hauled him away from the sick face. Yet Sandra Coffman still persisted in being pleasant.

"I've had a nice afternoon. I napped. It was very peaceful. But I'm clogged up awfully with this allergy."

"Allergy? You have a cold," Bernard said. "Catarrh! You are very sick."

"No. It's something on this table. Or in the room. Simone wiped the garlic off last night, but I keep getting so . . . so . . ." She started the spasmodic inhalations that precede a sneeze. Bernard, standing near her, backed away from the table. Strangely enough, the sneeze itself was weak, with a tiny little screech suffixed to it.

"Catarrh."

She sniffed. "Allergy," she said. "There is something in this room."

When Bernard and Simone climbed into bed that night, the conclusion, if not purpose, of Sandra's visit was known to both of them. She would die, perish before their eyes, and soon.

"Tomorrow," Bernard said, "you will leave with Karl very early and return as late in the afternoon as possible. I would prefer the evening. Feed him; take him to the films."

"We have very little money for that."

"Spend what we have."

"But what about the food?"

"Spend the money for the rent."

"But what about the rent?"

"Tomorrow you will leave with Karl very early. . . ."

Simone and Karl, dressed for the storm, left in the morning. Bernard remained behind to see Sandra through her last day. He was not quite so harsh with her now that the house was empty. One reason was that she was almost unable to speak. At times she was delirious, and her speech enchanted him. She lectured in whispers on the various ways peanut-butter sandwiches could be made—with bananas, some kinds of pickles, certain cheeses, and even candy. "I love the shore off-season," she said. "Ride like the wind," she said, repeatedly. "Ride . . . like the wind!" She sang "Bitter My Heart" several times. Hoarseness improved her voice slightly. The song itself remained ridiculous.

He did wipe her nose! And he wrapped a towel over her head and around her neck. You can imagine how difficult these acts were for him. But that part of his solicitousness was owed to a sense of failure. If she perished here, as she seemed certain to do, Bernard would have dishonored his calling. He would have received no enlightenment. Here was a puzzle offering, to all appearances, no challenge, and yet he had not solved it.

Toward noon, as she grew weaker and he tired of listening to her breathing and occasional bursts of song, he called to her.

"Don't speak," he said. "Conserve strength. I have questions. I will frame my inquiry in such a way that you can answer with a simple yes or no. I suggest you blink once for the affirmative, twice for the negative. One is yes, two is no. Do you understand?"

She blinked once. She smiled, weakly, as if pleased with the game.

"First, I wish to eliminate causes. I will give you a list of institutions and individuals who might have sent you here. Perhaps to spy on me. In each case, the question is this: Did such and such an institution send you?"

She scowled and began to speak.

"Hush. Save yourself. Now then. First question. Were you sent by the immigration office?"

Two blinks. No.

"Any branch of secret service—CIA, FBI, or others?"
Two blinks.

"Any federal, state, or local government agency?"
Two blinks.

Had she been sent by an agency representing a foreign country—"foreign" meaning, in this case, country other than the United States of America or international agency affiliated with a country other than the USA?

He had to repeat the question. She blinked negatively. No.

She was not sent by any political body or pressure group which espoused anti-Semitism, Francophobia, anti-intermarriage, anti-intellectualism.

No.

"By any being or force which was considered by itself or followers to be supernatural? For example, by something or someone thought to be a god or godlike?"

No.

"Do you believe in God?"

She blinked once, unhesitatingly, proudly.

"Have met him, or it?"

A reluctant negative pair of blinks: No.

I am hurrying this, and skipping questions that referred to the "known universe, areas or bodies beyond the known universe, possible sources within the known universe which are not supernatural but lie outside the limits of present scientific comprehension."

It should be noted that Bernard was embarrassed by the range of his questions, even smirked when mentioning anything that involved the unknown. And he rephrased some questions carefully, to catch her in a falsehood.

He spent almost an hour on this inquiry, which he considered preliminary, and it so tired poor Sandra that she began to keep her eyes closed after an answer for lengthening periods. Finally she fell asleep.

Sandra began, in midafternoon, a scarcely detectable motion, which was to become more pronounced as the hours passed. It was a spiral swing; the top of her head began to rotate slowly, in a small circle, but the gyres increased in sweep. I am happy to say that Bernard was appalled, sickened, as the motion grew pronounced enough to shake loose the towel. There was also a sound added to the rasp of her breathing. Somthing crackled, making a noise of threads breaking. She was coming loose from the table.

The curtain formed by the towel often parts; human features—a chapped mouth, a cute nose, pinched eyes—appear and then are covered with the movement.

Each time the curtain parts he is reminded that *this is a human head!*

He cannot bear the sounds of Sandra's departure. I savor the moment in which he is speechless, consider it my triumph. But, to give him his due:

"I will not teach forever," he said, suddenly, beginning as if in answer to a question. "A man must have more than one career. I intend to *write*. Poetry. In Dutch. You would be surprised what a fine language it is. Many very fine writers, of whom you have heard nothing, are Dutch. I am very fond of the Dutch, and I . . . well . . . I . . . *share* with Camus the desire for a return to the poem of length. The lyric exhausts its use by its brevity. Criticism, not the verse itself, has elevated it. I will not write one single poem of less than . . . less than . . . let us say one hundred lines."

He was speaking to cover the sound of her breathing, emphasizing words not for clarity. He wanted to fill the silences. (He reveals what was said about him earlier. Sorry.) "No heroes. It goes without saying, of course, without question . . . *that* I will not permit it. You see, when my mother died, in Buenos Aires, but you know nothing about her! Well, she died, in Buenos Aires, and I was a student, and everything I read then, and for years to come, and she died after my father died . . . anyway, I kept finding that I was not studying history, you know, or mathematics. No! Rather, I was discovering what survived war. Numbers, for example, survived; maps and photographs, complete books. *All* survived. People had less chance than their concepts. This struck me as *perfectly* reasonable! *Perfectly. Yes!* I found that books collected ideas, and, in fact, plans for evasion, no matter what the subject. In the *simple* shyness of childhood I discovered *tactics* for survival. *Tricks!* I was for a time a great storehouse of information about Napoleon. I talked about him constantly. *Why?* you may ask. Because the history of Napoleon had *survived.* In order for it to *do* so, *living* people had to pass his history along to others. I believed, sincerely, so long as I retained some information of importance, *I* was less likely to perish. In other words, in *other* words . . ."

The towel fell from the head. Bernard gasped. Her face was like cloud; gray and uneven patches of cloud could have been passing beneath the skin, for the pallor was not constant. Her milky flush gave way to an ashen dullness. In an aghast expression, mouth and eyes were open, parched nostrils distended. Her head constantly defied gravity by not toppling. (Hers was a too delicate, too fragile, feminine neck to support the wildly swinging head.) In its forward motion, Sandra's nose almost bumped the tabletop.

Bernard stood suddenly. He crouched, staring at her, his arms thrust behind him. (Imagine a diver at the edge of his own swimming pool, about to plunge in, when he sees the shark's fin cutting toward him.) Every sentence below was bellowed at full voice.

"I too have a wife, a son! I cannot promise them one damned thing, not even my presence, tomorrow! No! Nor can I be sure they are here—to be here, I mean!

"How much then can I make of them, of myself, of anything? Shall I ask them to trust me? Shall I trust them? No! Impossible! Impossible!

"Every word I utter can be proved a lie! I have done nothing! To promise is to commit a crime! The worst crimes against man are the promises . . . are the promises which . . . those which hope . . . allow him to hope! It is a crime to . . . it is suicidal to . . . Sandra."

She made a sound, not a word, a hoarse croak. The final lunging swing to the right pulled her loose, and the force of the swing skidded her off the edge, so that she dropped onto the seat of a chair, still spinning, rolled off and dropped to the floor. She bumped against a chair leg, skidded about toward Bernard, and came to rest on a cheek.

He went to a cupboard, took out a shopping bag. He lifted Sandra into it, taking her by the wet hair. He was surprised by her weight.

If he was half the scientist he considered himself to be, he certainly would have inspected the base of that neck, to see how she had been fixed to the table. But he did not. He lowered her into the bag, placed several pieces of trash over her, selecting such garbage as would be difficult to trace to him or his household.

He was not at all careful, however. He went out into wind and rain with only a light jacket, hatless, wearing his shoes but no socks (he saved on socks while at home). Once the weather struck him and began its drumming on his paper bag, he became apprehensive. If the paper was soaked, came apart, and his "trash" fell on the sidewalk, his life would be ruined. He went directly to the corner of Avenue A, flopped the bag into a litter basket, turned, and walked home. He would have preferred to venture farther west a few blocks, but it was senseless and his ankles felt as if they were being gnawed alive by the wind.

So he went home, back up the four flights of stairs, to the place where he and his family expected some refuge, some degree of safety.

When Simone and Karl came home later that afternoon, Bernard was writing, seated at his desk. His hair was dry, his damp jacket had been thrown on the floor, and in the kitchen the towel that had covered Sandra during her last hours remained on the table. Simone picked up the towel, came into the bedroom, and took the jacket.

"Bravo," she said.

"Bravo, Papa," said Karl.

"Out. Out! Silence!"

Simone obeyed. But Karl stood and stared at him. Bernard wiped his nose, self-consciously, and glanced at his clothing. Nothing wrong.

"What is it? Go out. I'm working."

"Where is she?" Karl asked.

Bernard paused to frame his answer carefully. I think he should have been kinder to the child. To say she was in heaven would not have been so cruel. To say, simply, that she was dead would have satisfied the boy, and because most children his age cannot conceive of death, it might have sent him off merely perplexed, to be diverted by a search for a definition.

But Bernard Wein would not permit himself such kindness. He would have called it deceit.

"She is in the trash. With all the garbage. We must keep our cities clean."

And he laughed at that. His little, spaced teeth glistened. Proud.

ONE SUNDAY IN SPAIN

I

The knocker sounds once. The knocker is of brass, a cast hand, distinctly feminine, grasping a ball, which, at rest, leans against a plate bolted to the door. Flipping it up and letting it fall of its own weight fills the house with an explosive crash.

Millie jumps. She stands still in the kitchen, hears her husband's feet whisper overhead as he treads lightly to the front balcony. A shutter squeaks open.

"Damn." She is making coffee.

"Mill-lay?"

She goes to the foot of the stairs. Andrew Devlin stands at the top, wearing undershorts. He is not a sleek man, and wastes little time in the sun. Furthermore, the patches of fur on his body are bleached a dull gray. She is astonished to see this. Then she smells orange blossoms. *Pulvos higiénicos*, his favorite talc.

"That was Mooney."

"So?"

"You're meeting him on the beach? He had his towel."

"If he goes to the same beach, and I see him and he sees me, and we want to talk, then we'll meet."

"I don't want you screwing around while I'm gone. I've told you that."

"You have. And I ignore it. I ignore you. You drunk. Crying and banging your fists on the wall. And screaming in the middle of the night. Calling me 'whore.' Crying! Don't tell me how to act, Andy. Don't tell me anything. Don't talk to me. You look awful in that powder. And your face looks boiled."

He disappears quickly through a doorway, into their bedroom.

II

Dressed now in a tweed coat, dark jeans, and new Spanish boots, Andrew is not greatly improved. He has spent several minutes angling that blue beret, knotting the silk scarf around his neck, getting the lenses of his dark glasses clean. He has oiled and combed his beard. He sits astride a Lambretta, parked before the door, checking his wallet for passport and money with very shaky hands. (Those small sores on the fingers? Burns. He doesn't smoke well when he drinks.) His eyes, behind the glasses, have a pulpy look about them, as if they'd been stepped on. He is tired.

"You've got to eat. I've got rolls heated."

"As you have said, time after time, I'm getting wine fat. I'll pass the rolls."

"Have you your other glasses?"

"I don't need them." He kicks the starter.

"Where are they? I'll get them."

"Don't need them." The engine catches. He smiles. He is somewhat concerned with the spectacle they make on Calle Franco at this hour. Only women coming late to mass, and a few men who have been out in the campo scratching at family gardens, are present to form opinions. Still, Andrew is sensitive.

"Don't be an ass. You'll wreck if you can't see."

"No. Don't worry about me. Take care of yourself."

"If you are worried, you can go to the beach with me."

"No."

"Well, let me get your glasses."

No. Again. He nudges the scooter off the stand, engine idling, warming up, and coasts down Calle Franco.

It's the last time they'll part in this world.

III

Millie finds the clear glasses minutes later. She looks over his room occasionally, when he's off somewhere, for the bulls or drink. He has a desk covered with notes and pieces of manuscript and books. There are dozens of ball-point pens and bound notebooks. There are coffee cups and ashtrays. He is engaged in writing a dissertation on the modern theater, its origins and inclinations. (Tentative title: *Hamlet Is Dead.*) But if one is half as shrewd as Millie, one will find in this scholarly disorder signals of Personal Chaos. Dead moths and cigarette ash, struck-through paragraphs on pages of fair copy, marginal notes, such as "Shit!" and "Presumptuous!" And street dust, a thin coating, over all. What does he do in here, day after day, while she's at her leisure with a vengeance?

The glasses are under notes toward his bold "*Introduction: Horatio Mounts the Stage.*" Here Andrew Devlin speaks through the suicidal king-maker Horatio, the good man who must live and proclaim Fortinbras king. What does Horatio think of kings and countries at this point? Andrew is struggling to discover. He has written in a margin: "Rethink that beginning line." ("I couldn't carry him. Too heavy and too wet with death.") He has tried: "If I wish to die and must live, and he loved life and died, who is left to speak here? Were his instructions his or a dying man's? And can I, a dead man, be trusted to utter what I did not—could not —hear?"

There are a dozen possible openings.

Millie doesn't read them now. Instead, she finds Andrew's glasses, in their case, the right lens only half there, cracked down the center, ruined.

Andrew, two nights before, and a bit tight, tried a handstand in the hall. No luck. And glasses are of no use in a handstand.

Millie places them—but not the case—on the table in the dining room. She wants them out in the open for her husband's return.

IV

He encounters the first omen. Jen Mooney, with her two sons, is out for a walk this morning.

"You look beautiful," she says, and she means it. "Look at him, boys."

She is very tall and handsome; the boys are handsome; the three beam at Devlin. They make him feel wretched.

"Going in to see the bulls?"

"Yes. Come along."

"Can't. They've still got colds. Millie at the beach?"

"No. She's home. She'll go later."

"They are meeting, you know."

None of the men lingering before the Costa del Sol, and none of the people crossing the highway to catch a bus for Málaga, and certainly not the bearded drunk who serves as a porter, can understand a word she says. Yet Devlin looks down the incline to the river bed, and beyond it to the fields of cane, with a certain longing.

"I trust Millie."

"You said differently the other night. When you were drunk." She shrugs.

He shrugs. Because he was. . . .

"Your house will be empty all day."

"So are the fields around here."

"But if you stayed here, with them?"

"No." He says that forcefully enough. She accepts it. She tightens her grip on the boys, and that's almost it.

Not quite. When he goes by her, he is a bit awkward. He nods as he passes and—goddamn!—the glasses slide down his nose. He reaches for them. *Idiot!* The scooter veers into mid-lane. He catches it before the oncoming bus . . . but if . . .

"Careful!" Jen screams.

He shrugs, unable to look back, and accelerates. Down the curve to the bridge, over the lumpy bridge, out across the countryside. The wind at his jacket; the cane leaves scrapping at the edge of the road. A little breeze. In the ring, wind is disaster.

V

She takes another coffee under an umbrella at Bar Alhambra. She is demonstrating a lack of compulsion. Then, just for a while, she strolls up and down the plaza, peering over one side at Calehonda beach. Nets dry there; fishermen sleep in the shadows of their boats, fully clad, flies at lip and nostril.

She partakes of the natural beauty; the sweep of coast toward Motril with its towers and winking rocks, and the blue Sierra Almijara. Phoenicians, Greeks, Carthaginians, Romans, Visigoths, Moors—all loved Andalusia. Who would not? Winter is unknown on the Costa del Sol, where the mean temperature is 54° F. while in the summer, cool sea breezes maintain a pleasant 70° F. Swimming year round. Come for fun.

The plaza ends in the surf, but above it, for it is on a rocky shelf said to have been part of a Moorish castle. The *ayuntamiento* is on one side of the square; the bars Alhambra (for the rough trade and permanent guests) and Marisol (posh, complete with Scopitone and clean-shaven lazzarone) face it. Date palms run out to the end of the square on one side, come back on the other.

This is where the *paseo* is held in the evening.

VI

Devlin does not stop in Torre del Mar, at the bar of Pepe, fattest bar owner in the area, because he is too late already. Damn near noon. And he has to see something, to justify this early departure.

Also he is wary of Pepe, who is a friend when the bar is empty except for Andrew, and a smug, silent pig when there are fishermen at the bar, drinking, eying the bold *extran-jero* in a fly-benighted looking glass.

VII

Behind the church a smaller square and, leading off that, a narrow way between two-story residences. Lingering here, at play on the air, are the stench of sewage and radio music. She walks through *cante hondo*, a thin falsetto voice delivering intricacies of woe. The doorways are draped. The wind blows back the drapes on marble tile and cats asleep on cool stone.

There is a turnoff to a walled lane where dirt floor, rotting walls, and the strenuous sun exchange potentials like elements in an electron tube. (She dampens quickly; her things grow moist.)

The wall ends on a blasted sugar mill. A burro with festered eyes grazes the ruined garden. Beyond the mill's yard Millie descends to the beach on a spine of rock, treacherous with fresh donkey droppings, falling away steeply to a tomato field. The field and the sand are separated by a canebrake, and through it one sees the white sand. She goes down, a gingerly but sure-footed young woman in new blue *alpargatas*, a printed orange dress without sleeves. Her hair is braided and bounces its final pennant just above her buttocks.

As she jumps down into sand at the base of the rock, Clement Mooney, the noted young Irish author, raises himself from his towel and darts toward her. The trot is no small tribute; it's hot.

"You look like the queen of the gypsies."

"I am."

He takes her basket. They are the only bathers on the beach.

VIII

Phoenicians, Greeks, Visigoths, Moors . . .

Andrew Devlin scoots the fertile coast, scarf-end popping near his ears, sorry he has not eaten.

The bulls excite him but so does hunger. As he drives, he kills his share of bugs, gathering them up in the thick folds of his jacket. They splash into the tweed; dry an instant later; and the wings and hard shells blow away. A few hit him in the face and sting. Let them choose another hour for crossing the highway. They endanger him. Let them die.

He regrets nothing. He leaves his wife to herself. I must be alone, he thinks. "Hamlet is dead" roars in his ears, roars like the wind when he is traveling, and roars in silence when he is not.

I cannot save what I cannot claim. The hero died quoting his best, most accurate poetry. I am here, measuring what devotion I have left, uneager to squander it on another person.

I may participate but I will not believe.

IX

She changes under a towel, one of many liberties the guests allow themselves. It is a process that requires squirming, a show of silken gear, some late adjustments. Mr. Mooney, watching intently, decides he would do well to swim when it is over.

Then they lie, side by side, on spread towels, sweating.

He reads. She watches fireworks swarm on the backs of her closed eyelids, thinking of Mooney, who had to go swimming. He has his hair cut by his wife because he cannot look in a barber's mirror. His beard clipped and shaped— a vain beard. He is lean, without excess though not muscular, coppery-colored except for the freckles, which are caramel-colored. He has the most remarkable nose. Quite long, very straight and thin. Blood seems to collect in it, near the bottom, just enough to tinge it pink. Once it is established that he does not suffer from a protracted respiratory ailment, his nose becomes quite an attractive feature. Very delicate. Like a rabbit's. Nostrils that seem to pout at times; at other times to flare joyously.

"We could go to your house for a while."

"We couldn't. Everyone in town knows Andy has gone to Málaga."

"Let me remind you that these people are here to provide a backdrop before which we dawdle, lasciviously."

"You are a snob bastard."

"I am a poor bastard, strongly taken by your principal parts."

He knows nothing of these parts, as yet. The closest to them he comes is just now, when she hands him the blue plastic bottle. He squeezes the bottle; there is a spitting sound.

"Curds. Concupiscent curds, as your Mr. Stevens would have it. That famed, unanguished poet."

The lotion goes into her skin cold, heats up immediately. His finger tips tour her back, bumping the borders of the suit, lingering in the hollows under her arms. She giggles, turning over.

"Oh, you'll never be fat!" he says, and goes off to swim.

X

The *sorteo* is over; the bulls are safely stored now, under the arena, in dark boxes they will occupy for most of their last afternoons as bulls.

Andrew parks alongside the reeking public toilet just outside the corrals. He charges up the stairs, against the flow of late-leaving spectators. He jerks off the jacket/charnel-house as he runs. The people coming down are troubled by his appearance. He is undaunted. He charges through mounds of swept-up peanut shells to the arches.

Below him are the pens, divided by walls, the tops of which are catwalks for animal handlers. A few men stand idly on the walls. One, that graying fellow in short sleeves who so resembles the late Hermann Goering, will appear this afternoon, pouchy in his suit of lights, as a peon in the fight. The rest, the remaining few, are unknown to Devlin. None of the young killers is present. And all the bulls that will perform that day are gone.

None of the certain doomed or the possibly doomed then. But, as has happened for the last two weeks, he does see one bull isolated in a pen where the steers are kept. This wild beast stands in mid-area, his face lifted so his short snout takes the sun evenly. Flies halo his head. Standing there, still as stone, but for the tail quirting the air above the befouled hips. A web of colorless slime depends from his nostrils. And facing that head, those sleepy eyes, are pale steers browsing the straw-and-dung floor of the pen for a bite of food, but watching their betesticled brother throughout the snack warily.

Devlin views the single bull as a latter-day Shelley might remark his moon. Why did the beast remain here, week

after week? Sick? Aged? Crippled in shipping? Is he a spare?
No! No simple answers.

He has either (a) so honored his kind that the crowd
has spared him; or (b) he is so dangerous, such a crasher
of gates and steer mauler when the pressure's on that he
has been quietly withdrawn; or (c) he is a fate-protected
entity which, in each drawing, is left behind as a substitute
for the coward; or (d) he is cowardly beyond redemption
by insult or injury, less than a steer, an absolute disgrace,
a male cow.

XI

The beach opposite the old mill ends on a point where an
old tower has fallen to rubble and a new, small shack for
the Guardia Civil has been erected. The point is connected
to the mill by a path which goes behind the tomato patch.

Perhaps this is confusing. Suppose you are offshore one
hundred yards, facing the beach. On your left, the broken
stone walls and the new shack. Then the beach, three
hundred yards, shaped like a quarter-moon. Then the rocks,
the outcropping that Millie walked down, and the old mill.
Directly behind the beach, and behind that thin fringe of
cane, are the tomatoes. Behind the tomatoes, up a bit, for
the tomato field was hollowed out by the sea, is the path,
running parallel to the beach.

Jen Mooney comes over the saddle next to the guard's
shack, carrying the smaller boy. The other is ahead, sitting
down at the top of a rocky slide; he bumps down on his
rump.

"For the love of Jaysus, will you look at that?"

Millie smiles, for her eyes are closed and she has just

turned toward him on the towel. She thinks he refers to her principal parts. But he trots off, kicking sand. He runs directly to the boy who slid and scoops him up. He carries the child up to the top, plants him beside the mother, and stands with his family. In very few minutes, in no time, really, Jen starts along the path to the mill, holding both boys by the hands. Very tall, she is, with the raincoat fanning behind her in the breeze.

Mr. Mooney does not return to the towel. He goes swimming. He swims out at an angle from the shore, and back at an angle to a spot even with Mrs. Devlin. The geometrical seducer. That swim takes about ten seconds longer than Mrs. Mooney's walk behind the tomatoes to the mill, and beyond the mill to the walled lane. Out of sight.

XII

For every beer you drink across the street from the arena you get, free, three cold shrimp as *tapitas*. They are not large shrimp. But nine hold Andrew's hunger in check for his scooter ride into the city. He is thinking of *gambas al pil pil* at Bar Baleares. And that rarity on the south coast, draft beer, warm itself but served in cold steins.

There is something to be said for drinking in the afternoon. The imagination unfolds early. The common cigarette tastes better than ever. The bones of the skull, particularly those of the frontal wall, cool, or seem to cool, by several degrees and sometimes quiver pleasantly.

Devlin stands at the bar, his feet in shrimp shucks, smoking his Celta, thinking of a little chapter on bullfighting. Or perhaps he could stitch bullfighting into chapter two, as yet unwritten, but beautifully entitled: "*Enter Giovanni with a*

Heart upon His Dagger." He is determined to make that the most important stage direction in history; to hell with the silly business of being chased by a bear.

XIII

"What did you tell her?"

"Take them away. The boys have been sick for weeks. Endless colds."

"She knows better than that. You shouldn't have sent her off."

"You are undone, huh?" He smiles, slaps water from himself. He does it to keep towels dry. "She knows a bit, and so does your husband. She mentioned it this morning, when she saw him going off. He almost killed himself after they spoke."

"He has no reason to worry."

"No. I suppose not. And she has no reason to come sneaking down the river bottom, bringing the boys through slime. Expects to find me with my incisors lodged in your thigh. Where they should be, mind you."

She has her eyes closed. When he places his big toe on her thigh, the sand's rough texture is toothlike, and she leaps up. "Damn you!" she shouts.

But he is drying his face, and his towel covers it, so she does not know if he is laughing. Or if he touched her on purpose.

"You are what is called, in the endless novels of sensitive American adolescents, a cock tease. Or a prick tease."

"Yes."

"And Andrew has nothing to worry about?"

"Nothing."

"Do you want me to leave?"
"No."

XIV

On Calle Larios, midway between the paseo and the Plaza Antonio, a club is located. Through broad windows of what might have been a department store, the stroller with an eye for curiosities will see, within, a seeming multitude of old men, seated in chairs of all conceivable shapes; and Andrew Devlin has decided that here, on this placid, prosperous street, are El Caudillo's chums, the castrating victors, killers of Lorca.

They are just men, but some are oddly dressed. Bars of light—sunlight broken by Venetian blinds—fall upon watch fobs and stickpins, upon great tufts of black handkerchiefs, on small black mourning flowers tucked in buttonholes, on hairpieces and gold-headed canes.

A C superimposed on an M mark it. On your right as you head toward the square.

XV

"I'm wrong. I have taken notes on you. You are not a tease. You are a nun in heat."

She says nothing.

"You know, they get a roving eye sometimes, the young ones. Particularly the schoolteachers. I think it's to scare up something for confession. 'He had tight trousers, Father, and his shins were hairy where they showed.' "

She forces back the smile.

"Are you writing now?"

"No. I make notes."

"About us, here?"

"Don't worry. If it gets into print I'll disguise you."

"How?"

"I'll make you and your husband symbolic. I'll give you Jamesian names. Mr. and Mrs. Waterproof Bandage."

XVI

He goes to the Bar Baleares, orders beer and *gambas,* pays before he is served, then goes down the street to Bar Pombo, for Bar Baleares has no facilities.

Here he orders a small Soberano—milder and more popular locally than Fundador—and slaps a *duro* down on the bar. He goes to the WC, relieves himself, returns, tips back the drink and leaves the change. He will not piss in one place, pay in another.

He returns to Bar Baleares, eats and drinks, orders a second beer, returns to Pombo, has *coñac,* returns to Baleares, more beer. So on.

XVII

She sleeps. He awakens her gently, by passing a hand over her face, blocking and unblocking the sun that strikes her eyelids.

"I' sooo sleeeeeepy." She awakens. "And lazy. Got to swim."

"Give me your hand."

Led, she goes directly into the water, but he returns for her cap. Salt water dries out her hair; the ends split and frizzle. And she does not like to wash it often, for it is slow to dry. Important, here, is this: She did not mention the swimming cap. He recalled it, stopped her before she got wet.

They wade out until the water comes up to her waist. She tucks her hair under the rubber, and gasps as the warmth of sleep washes off. The wind makes the water seem cold.

"Did you dream?"

"No. Yes. But I can't remember what I dreamed."

"Tell me your dreams. I'll get them published. *The Darty Dreams of Millicent D.* 'I'm walkin' O'Connell Street one recent mornin' when I meet a man with his member comin' straight out from the roof of his skull. So I says: You should wear a hat, sir, and no question. So he says: I tried it, ma'am. And, believe me, ma'am, it's a far greater shock when I doffs it.' "

She laughs long at that. And before she swims away she apologizes for being afraid. In the clearest statement of feelings she has made in the month Mooney has pursued her, she tells him this:

"I've been true to Andy when I haven't wanted to be. There was a man in California, where I worked. But I don't want to just give up. I've known you for a month and already I'm in trouble. It's trite, isn't it? The unemployed aliens abroad. I don't mean to tease. But I should be cautious."

"Mrs. Bandage thinks of the motives," Mooney says. "The motives and meanings. Do you know why I sent Jen away this morning, with her dear doe eyes brimming? Because I feel something being around you I don't often feel. That's all. I want feeling."

"I know. So do I. But what I feel like is a lazy American bitch."

XVIII

Then the *bodegas* down by the public market, in the alleys, where he samples wines that are all too sweet. There are three grades of the Tears of Christ wine in one bar, for instance, and all three are too sweet.

He buys peanuts and fills his beret with them, then goes about with the beret on his head until he comes to a *bodega*. He enters, puts the beret on the bar, and makes it clear that all comers are welcome. There are few takers.

He could kill Mooney right now; he could knock hell out of Millie as well. Similar ideas come to him between small glasses of sweet wine. But he discredits these dreams. This to be said about Andrew Devlin: When his confidence creeps out and attempts to invent the spiritual equivalent of Chellean I in a matter of seconds, his intellect races out, leashes it up before it hurts anyone. Sixty-seven units beyond the B.A. and seldom will a phrase such as "heart in mouth" apply to him.

Still, he's happy now. And this is the euphoria for which he drinks. Not only can he beat Mooney hand to hand, but he could, and he just might, turn out a little book that would sink Mooney's boat artistically. A little work on the so-called despairing novel. Tentative title: *Up from the Wasteland*.

This too: Some small bug, perhaps a fly, gets into one of Andrew's glasses of wine. He will not complain or ask for another glass. And he is too tight to sip around the fly, and too mannerly to lift the intruder out with a finger tip. So he drinks it down. Very likely in swallowing he imagines that Sartre or Dostoevsky or Antonin Artaud would have done the same.

XIX

They are late because the wind blows the sound of the chimes away from the beach, and they don't hear. (No one wears a watch.) They leave the beach. Both are sunburned and tired, and they have a fight. He wants to go to another bar, away from the plaza, because he wants her alone. He is carrying her basket.

She says she is still unable to sneak around as yet.

He says: "Don't accuse me of sneaking. I'm in hell's trouble with my family as it is."

She says she has heard of his past exploits (Mooney has lived in the village for over a year) and thinks Jen is probably accustomed to his adventures.

He says: "No one enjoys humiliation."

"Then you have been fooling around a lot?" She takes back her basket.

"For God's sake, will you remember you have not been here forever?"

They are ready to part, he for his home, she for the square, when he grabs the basket from her, this time burning her palms with the ropes that serve as handles, and strikes off for the square.

She has triumphed. She walks beside him, rubbing her hands, noticing how he strides like a chicken, his beaklike beard going forward and coming back with each step. She tells him this.

"I am not handsome," he says, turning to her, his beard angled loweringly, his nose fairly cringing.

"No," she says, always slow to flatter.

"God," he says, exploding laughter. "I don't know how a man can live with you. You have an uncanny knack for running no risk. You and your Hamlet-reheating husband."

Mooney hates a scholar.

XX

The wind will ruin the day. Andrew Devlin knows this. He brings his customary liter of *corriente* white wine, to share with the forthright, shy, noble, and friendly poor, with whom he sits, halfway up in the sun. He broaches the subject of last week's *novillada*. The bulls committed suicide. He speaks of last week's hero, El Terremoto de Torremolinos. That town cannot produce a man. The bulls were fond of him, but perhaps for an improper reason.

All agree the wind is very bad.

One of the sharers of the wine has something in the corner of his mouth. That could be a cold sore. Could be just chapped lips. After that man drinks, Devlin tries to interest others in the bottle.

He does not require much wine. He is drunk enough. He makes light of the aliens who fill the expensive seats, of the men who chase down rows of bleachers after the straw hats of their wives. And when one large-breasted Yankee girl in slacks drawn tight as a fist appears, looking for Lou, Andrew is just as quick to stomp his feet and howl as is Sore-lip. He is clapped on the shoulder numerous times. His wine goes the rounds.

But the wind will ruin it all. When the band starts, two *pasodobles* race inside the ring; one crisp and on key, the other flat and lurching. The flags above the president's box crackle—small arms in the distance.

XXI

The first mistake: arriving on the square during the quiet, apparently preoccupied moment after an argument. One effect of this: to walk by Jen's table without stopping. One of Mooney's sons sees his father, hails him. Jen has been watching the two intently. She is seated with Mr. Ruggles, the first new American in a week.

"Fancy your not seeing us," Jen says.

Women with large mouths seldom fake a smile convincingly.

"Why didn't you say something? What is this Mrs. Miniver business?"

"I believe you've met my husband, Mr. Ruggles?"

"Yes. Two nights ago. At the Bar Crucero?"

"Antonio Three's place," Jen corrects him.

"Oh, yes. Antonio Three's."

"Mr. Ruggles," Mooney begins. "Where do you purchase trousers like that? Did you have them made up? And the shirt as well. I've never seen such fancy stuff."

Ruggles' clothing is ordinary enough. Mooney is simply after him. He's tall, he's an unshy American, and he carries a new Hispano Olivetti portable down to the plaza some mornings, to do his writing in the sun.

"Mr. Ruggles," Jen says, "met Andrew last night. Andrew was quite drunk. He told Mr. Ruggles you were a fine writer, Clem." She turns to Millie. "Do you think you could tell Andrew, Millie, not to boast for Clem so? It seems a little funny to some people, I'm sure. He has such faith, you know. It just never quite occurs to him that—"

"Will you shut that great big bloody gob of yours before I ram this beer bottle down it?"

Jen and Millie laugh at Mooney's extravagance. Ruggles, who is already starting his beard, scratches at the sketchy growth and grins.

Mooney continues: "And those shoes as well. Schooners, made out of chamois. With soles of paralyzed foam off a pint of Guinness. What would a pair like that cost in sterling? Could you figure that out for me?"

Poor Ruggles scratches and converts. Jen tries to interest Mooney in other matters. In the sound of three hundred people walking on the square in early evening. In the scent of inexpensive perfume and smoke from a fire under a cauldron of hot oils, into which coin-shaped cuts of potato are tossed by a gypsy girl. The smoke is rosemary smoke, almost as fragrant as the perfume. Mooney interrupts her.

"They tell me you are an artist."

"I thought I'd try to do some writing while I have the time. And the money." He laughs and sucks his teeth.

It is a stupid answer. Jen shrugs and withdraws, taking up a cigarette and nudging Ruggles for a light.

"The whole bloody coast is bulging with Americans like yourself, so rich they feel they're gifted," Mooney says, beginning quietly. "Idiots. They haven't read anything but bank books. They come and they carry brand-new type-writers with them, and they write every day for a week, and the rest of the time they sit about telling other Americans what a good thing they've got going for them. I've seen some of the shit they stick to paper. He fucks her on the last page. It's oriental and Buddhism and co-ordinated orgasms. They have orgasms to rival the eruptions of Vesuvius. We see them in the last sentence floating off to paradise on scalding sperm, happy as pigs in shit. *Pigs in shit*, Mr. Ruggles. I hope you have something else in mind."

Mooney almost collapses onto the table when he finishes. Poor Ruggles has left off scratching. Mooney looks at him as if he has come here to see Ruggles die.

"I'll tell you how to write, Mr. Ruggles," Mooney says, slumping in his chair, white in the face and beard bent against his chest. "Kill yourself doing it."

Ruggles pays soon and leaves. He pays for everything. He leaves a tip, which Mooney pockets while his wife calls him an ass in a dozen different ways.

"I suppose," he says to Millie, intentionally shutting up Jen, "I suppose you think that man is handsome? With his handmade trousers and bog-water eyes?"

"No. Of course not, I—"

Jen jumps up. "What? Do I hear correctly? Was that all a lover's quarrel? Are you jealous, Clem? Right here? Before me?" Her lips, drawn over her fine teeth, are white. She wears no lipstick. "I *must* go!"

She does go. She calls the boys, who are playing among the legs, and they walk off. From the rear, and seen moving away in the raincoat, Jen is man-sized. Her appearance, quantitatively taken, makes her less pitiable. It's a shame. The wives of poor artists often deserve pity. They cannot achieve fashion, the very thing that makes other misused wives so unpitiable. Jen is crying. She holds her head up, and the tears roll out along her lashes.

XXII

The trumpet, then the bull. Andrew cannot see it come from the *toril*, which is almost beneath him, to his left. This is a good moment for Andrew, in spite of the wind and the dust. There is a good deal of unspecified lust in the young man. Sun, wine, danger (for someone else) can stir him to exhilaration. He begins to sweat profusely, and one cheek twitches.

The animal is a feast for the eye. He trots out, head up, alert and jumpy. He goes to the center of the ring and sidesteps a complete circle, looking over the crowd.

Three peons come out into the ring and shake capes at him. He continues to look at the stands. One opens the cape and trots out nearer the bull. He lowers his head; the man drops one side of the cape and walks away from the bull, dragging the cloth. The bull lifts his head. Not going anywhere. Andrew's questions here are always the same: Is he a coward or wise? Does one quality imply the other?

Antonio Medina comes from behind the barrier, his serious long face going one way and his serious long hat going the other. He has his cape folded before him; when he straightens it out, he takes the top of it between his teeth. It opens like a sail. He approaches the animal.

Nothing.

He tries several times striking a toe into the dust, grunting. Then tries to lead the bull to another spot. Then tries a new angle; this seems to be the answer. The bull starts. But in mid-charge he veers off and gallops around the outside edge of the ring, looking up into the stands.

Medina seems to know where the bull will stop. He goes there; it is almost as far from Andrew as he can go and remain in the ring. He sets himself, and the bull comes for him; he makes the one good pass of the afternoon.

Sore-lip slaps Andrew on the back and pulls the bottle out of his hands. "That Medina, a good man, eh?"

Andrew cannot tell if that spot is open or just discolored. In size, color, and texture it suggests a raisin. Another Gregor Samsa? Perhaps Sore-lip was at one time an insect? And his humanity just a rotten trick someone had played?

Andrew expands on this, juggling ideas a bit, so that Horatio and Hamlet are included, while the horses enter the ring.

XXIII

"Mad bastard! You have no right to be jealous! And you are an idiot, talking like that before your wife."

"You'll have to take care of me tonight. Feed me. She'll lock me out."

"I'm serious. You've ruined everything."

"I'm serious. I have been all along. I've ruined nothing. Yet."

"But you just said she would—"

"—Lock me out for an hour, or five hours, or a night. A single night at best. She depends on me, you know. I am her provider and protector." He speaks without humor. "She, in turn, is the mother of my sons. Our union has purpose."

"If that's the case, why—"

"—Why do I try to lure the likes of you into the cane fields? Surely all of Andrew's talk about plague and hubris and absurdity has convinced you that man is imperfect?" No irony there; he would guard against it.

She will not tolerate unkind comments about her husband most of the time. She is beginning to admire Mooney as a domestic acrobat. What risks he runs, she thinks. For me, she thinks.

XXIV

The third bull of the afternoon gets a horn in between the

legs of Earthquake from Torremolinos and lifts him high over his back, a garish horizontal figure in green and gold —and hat—above the bull's broad back suspended, wriggling. Andrew Devlin feels that blow to the groin. He gasps and his knees fly apart. Then the bull lowers Earthquake to his feet and extracts the horn from a two-ended tear in his trousers. The young man is, however, not unscathed. Blood trickles out; a patch of blood widens and lengthens on the satin; in a while it will tint the hose. But a little wound is not enough.

The wind blows off all chance for glory. Nothing can be glorious in the old sense. Define the word anew. He is disposed to wring from this moment new ideas for his volume, but he is troubled by the drunkard's quick-fill bladder. So he misses the new glory of a too-early, too-eager kill and passes down between the rows of troubled knees to the aisle. Downstairs, in the bowels of the arena, he finds a public room—fetor, muddy floors, savage flatulence.

This should be on stage as well, he thinks. Should be up there, on display, wounding the senses, this rankling commonplace. For is it all not, even on the sunniest of days, a shit heap getting higher for the good weather?

Light—splinters of it, coming from cracks in the seats— and the mumble of voices, like the groan of happy, harvesting bugs gloating over a clover field or a cadaver. And off a bit, a horse's weak whinny, cockcrow of this underworld. Andrew, returning, is almost merry.

XXV

It is arranged, then, in the oddest fashion. She has no money; he never has money. She must go home because she has been too long at this bar and she wants a shower. He will leave with her, but he will have no place to return to, since he has chased his wife off, and the other foreigners do not, as a general rule, like him. What will we do with him then?

Mind if I just sort of you know tag along kind of thing? Heh. Heh.

"There's some beer at my house," she volunteers. Not just consent, mind you, but a show of undisguised zeal.

They cross the square, right through the *paseo*, her head high, on a level with any inquisitive head turned toward her, providing the backdrop, as he said, for their dawdling, as he said.

He carries her basket.

Passing Antonio Cerezo's bar, they see Mrs. Mooney and her two boys. She is seated at a table; the boys are beneath the table, sipping orange Fanta. And Mr. Ruggles, fingers combing the whiskers, is entertaining.

"He must be the host. Jen would never buy them Fanta."

Millie sees them, says outright: "What if she takes a liking to Mr. Ruggles? What if they became lovers?"

"I would be surprised."

"But . . ."

"I couldn't stop her. And I would not hate her for it."

Yes, Millie thinks. "Andrew," she says, "feels differently."

"Andrew does not enjoy himself at anything. Candy exists to rot teeth. Books exist to reveal heresy. Wives to ruin husbands. And on. And on."

They turn into Calle Franco. It is dusk and the slot of the street runs shadow and human forms. Without the street lights it is very dark, a flooded river bearing away a populace. But the tops of the buildings on the right-hand side still hold some sign of day to them. There is a remnant of light along the fringe of tiles that overlaps the walls. And the faces of the gargoyle rain pipes—serpent and beaked bird—angle their rusty menace out over the dark movement below.

Mr. Mooney takes the keys, opens the door.

XXVI

Andrew begins to drink beer. He buys beer for his friends, the cohorts of Sore-lip, who could not afford a chancre, and they continue to slap him on the back and consult him about the matters of the *corrida*. Their slurred speech and his stumbled hearing produce intimacy.

The last bull of the afternoon is Earthquake's. For almost every person present it has been a dismal day; yet, because Earthquake was last Sunday's hero, there is some hope left. Fewer people are leaving than one might expect. Still, enough go to indicate a bad day, and enough of these are Spaniards to certify the failure.

Earthquake sends everyone out of the ring and then is chased out himself by the bull. He goes headfirst over the barrier. But no one finds this funny. There is a reason: the bull shows courage. None of the capework is of exceptional quality, but there is just the faintest suggestion that the failure is now due to the whims of nature (the wind). The wind has been diminishing steadily for some time. But it is still there. There is some anger when the change is ordered by the president.

XXVII

It is not quite a kiss. When is a kiss not a kiss?

He takes her in his arms but he bites her. Bites the lower lip, and hard enough to set her hopping in pain.

She *loves* it. Brute. *Brute.* Animal!

"Just a minute," she says. And she rushes upstairs to her bedroom for her contraceptive equipment. (The pill makes her ill.) In a minute she returns prepared.

Descending the stairs she notices how, in an odd way, that pain in her lip has become something less than pain. It is a tingle, very slight. But when he kisses her again, she knows the truth: that lip is swelling. Still she is far too aroused to let a little swelling stifle a pure passion.

They "sink to the floor" after bumping around in the dark, knocking against the table. (It is a shame, in a way, that Andrew's broken glasses did not fall off that table, break completely, for the symmetry.) She is bitten a few times; ear lobes and lower neck, shoulder, lip again. The biting is a bit extreme, she feels, as it goes on. She worries about marking. A swollen lip is one thing; appearing nibbled up quite another. This worry, and it really reaches its peak after coitus, probably is the single unpleasant aspect of their intercourse, but it deprives her of orgasm. Mooney, however, finds nothing in his way.

XXVIII

With the small cape Earthquake might have saved the day. But the pics have ended the fight for him, as they often do when young bulls show courage going after the horse. The wind cannot blow away the horse, as you might suspect, and if the bull looked indecisive or handicapped in the phase previous, he is now able to display his power and determination against insane odds.

So the crowd cheers the bold animal as he impales himself, and the president is reluctant to send the horses out, and it goes on a little—perhaps only one gouge—too long. Earthquake is furious and shows it. When it is time to kill, he does not dedicate the bull. He walks from behind the barrier dragging the *muleta* and approaches the animal with his hands at his sides. But he gets close. And in his stride is a bit of a swagger. When he flashes the cape and the bull's head lifts quickly, following the cloth, the young man sees that the vision is impaired not at all. No, what has ruined this bull is the blood lust of the audience. Earthquake manages to communicate this with a contemptuous shrug.

He lifts the cape then. And the bull lurches forward and knocks the young man down. It is more on the order of an enforced nudge. Earthquake plays dead. The bull doesn't give him a thought. The crowd enjoys this.

He is bowled over three times. The beast does not seem concerned with hurting him. Disgrace him, yes; but wound him, never.

Andrew grasps that. Others—howling now—do not. Andrew wants to see it. It helps him, gives him strength, affirms.

XXIX

She takes a shower and does one or two other little things to her person. Mr. Mooney waits for her, first in the kitchen and then in Andrew's study, where he is not permitted.

He is drinking a beer and looking over Andrew's papers when Millie comes in. She is barefoot, wears white slacks and a shirt with the tail out. Her lip is swollen and there is a strange mark on her neck, just below her left ear.

"What are you doing in here?"

"Drinking my beer, looking for a match, and sneaking glimpses of your husband's notes. It is a very dreary room. No one could find a place to put an idea in all this."

He indicates the desk.

"From the looks of the dust I don't think he does much anyway," Millie says. A momentary regret, a small extravagance.

"You don't know?"

"No. He has quit typing. He thinks at one speed, types at another. So he says."

"The miserable bastard."

"It's a strange time to feel sorry for him."

"I don't care about him. I'm thinking of you." He looks at her. "That lip. He'll see that, you know. And the other thing."

She takes that lip in her fingers, tenderly. "The 'irst ti' I 'een 'itten."

Mooney's nose quivers; his spastic nostrils pale. He turns his head. "It's all damned cruel. We should all squeal like cats when we're at it. Just like a lot of cats."

XXX

He leaves when the bull is dying and Earthquake, dust-covered and muddy in places with sweat, is standing before the crowd, his hands before him, supplicating. He wants permission to circle the ring after the animal is dead. The

people are jeering, whistling. Sore-lip calls him shameless.
A man rushes out, digs a dagger into the bull's neck, and
the great hulk convulses, the eyes roll, the tongue emerges,
blue-black with death.

Devlin leaves.

He has a little trouble keeping the scooter upright and
under him while starting it. And the dark glasses bother
him more than they should.

Li'l coffee. Somethin' to eat.

Unfortunately, where he stops there is nothing to eat
but half a dozen churros that have spent the afternoon
blotting up oil from other churros that have been sold.
Soggy rolled dough fried in fat and chill now, just a trifle
rancid. There is one cause for his eating what little he
eats. The woman who sells him the coffee has three fingers
missing from one hand, is ugly, and runs a dirty little coffee bar. She is quite apologetic when he asks for something to eat. All she can offer him is this handful of
churros. But she will give these to him. Por nada. But,
but. No, señor.

Gracias.

XXXI

Ruggles and Jen and the children, all clamoring at the
door. And Mooney lets them in. The idiot. Millie retreats
to the kitchen, where she begins slicing fresh tomatoes for
Andrew's salad.

Jen and Ruggles are a bit tight. The children come in
and stand against the wall. They are tired. Millie would
like to offer the children some milk, but she cannot turn
to them because her swollen lip would be exposed.

"Clem, I want you to apologize to Mr. Ruggles here. He is a very fine young man who has done his level best to keep down venereal disease."

"I'm very sorry. And thank you," Mooney says.

"Did you *hear* that, Millie? He fights venereal disease. He is a civil servant, and he goes about Los Angeles tracking down syphilis. He is hell on the homosexual; dreadful carriers, that lot. Promiscuous."

"I'm the curse of the spirochete," Ruggles puts in.

"He calls himself the syph-hound. Millie? The syph-hound?" Jen stops talking for a second. Millie, who isn't looking at her, cannot look at her, senses the trouble.

"Syph-hound," she says, but too late.

Jen is upon her in an instant. "Turn around." She shakes her head. "Oh, God, it's done, is it? You poor thing; he's chewed you all up."

She goes away. She gets her children and Mr. Ruggles and starts out the door. Then she stops and leaves the children with their father. And she and Mr. Ruggles go out the door. And the boys look at Mooney and Millie.

"Hungry, Da," says one.

"Yiss," says the other.

XXXII

The dangers are not the roads themselves, which he knows well enough, but the towns where there are no plazas. Here the couples walk the highway, and try to get out into the darker places, near the fields. And the young men enjoy walking far out into the lane, so that cars have to swerve to miss them, for it is no small thing, moving a car out of its path with your mettle. No woman will deny that.

So he goes along successfully enough for a while. He gets sick once and has to stop and throw up. But that is not so bad. And when the headlights of a passing car illuminate a band of saliva that connects him with his vomit, he is not even ashamed. He knows the limits of man. They are writ broad upon the earth. He has spent the day studying them.

He decides he cannot stop for coffee again; in spite of the unpleasant prospects home affords him—Hamlet is dead; the palace is torn down; and Hamlet didn't work out well there anyhow—he must return to his house, his food, his bed. Tomorrow? Read Camus. Live for the moment.

Beyond Torre del Mar then, cruising through cane fields, killing bugs and tasting bitter, he is not an unhappy man. The chorus of dark and the stars; the wind blowing past his ears; the scooter's little drumming; the sickness abated —all conjoin to lift him above ordinary or embarrassing circumstance.

He goes over a bridge and makes a slow curve through the dark, so that, emerging from the shadow, lights of a roadside settlement appear. He cuts his speed automatically; and the generator puts out less power; and the cone of the headlight's beam is shortened.

Happens every day.

XXXIII

I am not going to be depressed, Millie thinks.

"Let's all eat together," she says. "Andrew will be here soon. I'll cook for all of us."

"What about your wound?"

"He won't think anything of it. I'll say I fell. Or a *cala-*

baza dropped down and hit me. The *calabazas* fall all the time out in the patio."

"I wouldn't believe that."

"What do you suggest?"

"That you tell him what happened."

"Why?"

"To see what he does."

She gives the boys slices of tomato. She is considering Mooney's statement. His proposal. Why this?

"Why?"

"Because he won't do anything."

"So?" She responds thus because she suspects that he is correct. She is a little shy confronting that suspicion. After all, she is married to the man.

XXXIV

First it is a dark shirt, white teeth, and a shoe getting into his beam. He merely turns and avoids the couple— the young woman's shriek is a beacon. In a hundred yards or so, he will be in the light of the village; he would not have had this difficulty, which was hardly a difficulty at this moment, had he been a hundred yards farther down the *carretera*. These are, however, his last one hundred yards.

In compensating for the abrupt turn, Andrew Devlin unwittingly alters the current of air that plays up over the front of the scooter. A bug, drawn to the diminished beam of his headlight, blows in, under the frames of his dark glasses.

One could call it the intervention of fate.

With one eye blind and the other burning, his first reaction is to release the clutch hand and rub the pain. He does this—idiot!—and the scooter swerves again. The second couple scream; he twists the wheel, this time in trouble, knowing it, and calm enough. He is slowing down. Tears are the hindrance; the lights come forward as through slime. Yet there remains to him a chance, but a slight one, as all must see.

A dog, a fat waddling long-dugged mongrel bitch, which feeds her litter from what refuse finds its way into the drainage trenches that border the road, misjudges the sound of his approaching scooter, the unsteady beam of his head-lamp. She undertakes to explore the other side, for the odd morsel, and trots across. She makes it, but the uproar that seems to descend upon her sends her rolling down into the ditch. She crawls up to the edge, she lays her nose on the cool gravel of the shoulder; she eyes the confusion she, in part, has caused.

For Andrew Devlin will harm neither the discreet lovers nor the chubby little mother. When the dog's crusty nose enters the cone of his light, he jerks the wheel again, double braking an instant later and squeezing the handbrake before he hits the pedal. The front wheel locks at an angle. The rest of the scooter rams up against the gooseneck, and the rear end lifts, throwing Andrew upward.

Here, for an instant, his new boots rise, heels together, hat and glasses still in place. With a boost from the machine, he has achieved his handstand. Right up, continuing after the rear tire drops, and just as he enters the glare of the town's first street light, he is complete. Doomed, absurd, comic, misunderstood, he is sailing down a Spanish road at some thirty miles per hour, upside down, as if the

greatest trick Lambretta rider of all time had arrived un-
expectedly, and now the sleepy little *pueblo* were in for some
real thrills.

But Andrew leaves the support of the handle bars, moves
onward, pulled downward, arms dangling, hands spread.
The illusion ends. He hits but is slow in tumbling. The
hat is scraped away, and it is not empty, and what it con-
tains is not peanuts. His body settles slowly. Brows, bones,
blood, tweed, buttons grind from the slow sprawl. The
scooter, wide open, spins in a circle, its light probing the
sky.

Spaniards keep the dogs off for a time. Then two members of the Guardia Civil arrive and order the men to
keep the dogs off.

They cover Andrew Devlin with a tarp.

XXXV

The boys eat sliced tomato, sucking juice from their fingers. They are seated in the hall on the floor, will not sit
at the table. Millie, using the ribbed skillet, will be serving
them fresh sardines à *la plancha* soon. Mooney will do his
best to remove the bones.

Millie is silent, and Mooney, always thinking for others,
thinks he knows what she is thinking.

"If you put a little ice on the wound, the swelling will
go down."

"Ice," Millie repeats, and leaves the stove for the icebox.

"Unless you've decided to tell him."

"I can't see why I should. If he won't do anything."

"Most likely Jen will tell him."

"He won't believe her."

"It would be better if he did. It would be more interesting. It would give him something to think about, something quite real." He walks to the stove, takes up the
spatula, flips over a fish. "Hamlet, you know, was a fic-
tional character." He smiles. "Wasn't he, boys?"

"Yisss."

And they are right, all of them, about everything.

SAILORS AT THEIR MOURNING: A MEMORY

One night in November, 1952, a Navy patrol aircraft crashed into a freezing sea a few miles offshore from the North Korean port of Wonsan. It was an old seaplane, a PBM, loaded down with electronics equipment, depth charges, and fuel for a full night of flying. It flew in over the task force that blasted North Korea from international waters, cruising at two thousand feet; one engine quit and the ship began to fall away to the powerless side.

There was probably time to jettison some fuel and arms, but there was not enough time to lighten the load so that a single straining engine could maintain air speed. According to men who had seen or experienced single-engine flight, the weak side would be low, and the ship would go into a descending spiral. When it hit, they said, the pontoon would catch the crest of a swell, pulling the wing tip under, and the aircraft would probably flop over on its back, break up, and catch fire.

Witnesses aboard a destroyer in the task force confirmed

the fire. They steamed up to it, skirted it looking for survivors; they searched through the night. They found nothing. By morning a storm blew up from the south, dispers-
ing the oil slick. There were thirteen officers and men
aboard.

The lost plane was one of twelve belonging to an anti-
submarine squadron that patrolled the east coast of Korea,
the Tsushima Strait, and the Yellow Sea from a base in
Japan. The squadron had arrived from the States only a
month earlier, and the sudden and complete disappearance
of one ship and thirteen men was an awesome thing for
some of us. I was a second radioman, radar operator, and
titular gunner on one of the planes. Like many of the
younger sailors, I had enlisted in the Navy so that I would
not be drafted into the infantry, and I had spent a good
portion of my enlistment in training schools. When I was
assigned to a flying outfit and managed to learn the Morse
code, I was given a chance to fly. It meant extra money
and an easy life. Air crewmen stood fewer watches and did
less work. I was not at all prepared for death.

There were older men in the squadron who warned us
that our planes were dangerous, untrustworthy always, absolutely defenseless against attack. (We didn't worry about
attack.) The squadron lost planes regularly. It spent eight
months in the States, training pilots and new men, and
six months overseas. Never in its history did a full cycle
of fourteen months pass without a crash, and never did
all the crew escape death.

But the men who admonished us were career sailors,
veterans of World War II who had developed those pe-
culiar enthusiasms and loyalties that permitted them to
make a life of the service. A few were sincere, hard-work-

ing, intelligent. Most of them were wretched men, good at their work, but their work was stupid.

The Navy, clumsy and official, tried to awaken in us a sense of purpose and an awareness of the threats. At briefing sessions before each flight the intelligence officer reported what enemy planes had been sighted. It was generally known then that the Chinese used the Korean War as an extension of cadet training.

On a huge briefing-room map of the area, circles were drawn over sections of seas. Grease-penciled into each section was the current water temperature and a translation of that into minutes that a man would survive if afloat there.

Once, I remember, we were told that, should we go down off Vladivostok, we would have something like seventeen minutes. The planes flew up that way for a weather check after leaving the task force, so it was not out of the question. But we didn't worry. We weren't going to cream in, but if we did, we would get into a life raft.

Some clear nights a jagged, self-sustaining lightning flash visible off the starboard wing marked the fire line of the ground war. Our boys were out there, American soldiers, dying in the snow for free men everywhere. They could have enlisted rather than wait out the draft. We had enlisted. It was possible to be prudent while assuming one's share of the national risk.

Only once in that orientation period were we confronted with the unquestionable proof that we were engaged in a deadly business. We had a lecture on survival in North Korea, delivered by a Lieutenant Commander Birdwell, who had volunteered to go behind the lines and do his best to open up escape routes for downed fliers. In the event that any of us went in near the mainland and decided to try our luck on foot, we were advised to stay close to the coast, avoid settlements, bribe farmers, and eat either cats or dogs—I cannot remember which animal was recommended.

The lecture should have been convincing, but Birdwell made it all seem like more propaganda. He had been burned terribly. His face was plated with skin grafts, none of them matching, and his hair was linty and grew in little bolls scattered over a tortured scalp. He had a tiny nose with unmatched nostrils, and his eyes peered out of rough, irregular sockets, like holes torn in a paper bag.

He was so disfigured, and so obviously delighted by some of his shocking counsel, that it was like that famous, unheeded VD film, where the man with advanced paresis, sitting in the wheelchair, kept trying to count to ten.

"If I looked like that," Kramer said, "I wouldn't eat dogs or cats."

We didn't listen; then the first plane crashed and the first men died. Three were officers, remote from us. Three or four were veterans. But the remainder were fine young men, like us.

The day before the plane was lost, my crew had flown out over the Tsushima Strait, a short gravy hop during which we photographed shipping. When we came home, we were pulled up on the seaplane ramp for minor repairs. We had liberty that night. As the storm front moved through, and two-boat was flying toward its doom, I went into the small town outside the gate, drank beer, and danced with bar hostesses.

The girls were perfect. They were humorous and gentle.

And they needed us. I had never been around a collection of pretty, young, intelligent girls who needed me—not as a civilian and certainly not as a sailor. It was a blessing, a whiff off a dream, and another eloquent argument against worry.

I came back to the barracks late, probably staggering, but damned happy, I'm sure. And there were all the men in the dorm, wide awake, dressed for flight. They sprawled about on the big picnic table, the single piece of unnecessary furniture in the room. They wore bulky winter flight suits and fleece-lined boots. They were silent; they all looked up when I walked in, grinning.

"'Bout time you got back," Pat Fanning, my plane captain, said. "Two-boat's missing."

Pat was another battered man. Once, not too long before I met him, the husband of the woman he loved had got him drunk one night and had almost killed him, laying him out first with a bottle and then kicking and stomping him. He came out of that with his face a fine mesh of scars. He had been handsome—he showed us photographs when he was on a friendly drunk—and now he was blurred and broken.

When he was full of contempt, which was his usual state, he could say "Two-boat's missing" and somehow imply that it would not be had I stayed on base and had the husband, a first-class storekeeper, not beaten him.

"Missing? Where? What happened? Who flies in two?" I was worried about friends first.

"Some poor bastards we'll never see again," someone said.

"Nobody said they creamed," Harper said.

"Listen, they don't put the whole outfit on standby if it's just radio failure. You'll see."

"Get your gear on," Pat commanded.

"I will. But who's in two?"

"Nobody we know," Kramer said, too loud.

"What do you mean you don't know them? They're your shipmates. You pukes don't give a damn about this outfit, do you?"

"I mean no one we know well."

Kramer, Harper, and I had gone to electronics school in Memphis. Scattered through the squadron were other classmates from whom we selected our close friends. All of us had at least started college, and Kramer had finished it. We talked a lot, and loudly, about our futures in the civilian world. We read books and criticized movies, and Kramer even went so far as to write poetry. We disturbed the atmosphere of the dorm. We were snobbish in a ridiculous way, but in the Navy it helped to feel superior to your superiors.

Kramer ticked off the names of the missing men while I pulled off and folded my uniform. I knew only one man well. He was a thin, nervous, bespectacled mech, who had a clear tenor singing voice. At squadron parties he and I and two men of the ground crew formed a quartet and sang barbershop music and college songs. I had gone off for beer a few times in the States with the metalsmith of the crew. The first radioman was a squadron legend. He was a devoted alcoholic with a tricky stomach. He could tell if his gut was up to boozing each morning when he brushed his teeth. On a bad day, toothpaste made him sick. In the head we could hear him retching and spitting. If he passed his toothpaste test, he would announce it.

"Made it, by God! Anybody want to go into town tonight?"

I dressed and stretched out on my bunk. The steam

heat had been left on, the suits were hot and heavy, and Pat told us to keep them on, allowed us to leave the zipper open, but that was it.

"If they call us, they'll want us at the hangar right now."

"If those guys crashed, by now they're frozen."

"The poor bastards."

"Aw, it's a radio. It's gotta be. It's just *gotta* be."

"It don't *gotta* be nothin'."

I was sleepy. I lay in the bunk, trying to stay awake, trying to remind myself that some men were missing, a ship might be down.

"'Member that time down in the Pescadores, Pat? When some dumb fuckin' radioman forgot to pull the control locks? Jesus, that dumb sonofabitch."

"The last locks he ever forgot to pull."

They talked of crashes; they always spoke of death.

I fell asleep.

We had three days of rain and wind in Japan, and the storm prohibited our searching for survivors. The bay that served as our airport was too choppy. PBM's were stubby-winged, heavy old ships with none of the grace of the more famous PBY. Swells of four feet or more were considered too hazardous for taking off and landing. We were grounded by weather, kept on standby, and restricted to the base. We could not leave the dormitory without informing our plane captains of our destination. The three captains, all of them first-class mechs, ruled off sheets of stationery and made check-out lists the first morning.

"You people know what this list is. This here list is a list for you people to check out on. Any sailor moves his ass out that door for anything that takes longer than it takes to crap had better get his name down on this list. You people know we're on standby and that some poor fuckin' shipmates may be out there freezin' their asses. . . ."

I remember those three days as dark and wet, with the wind grinding on the barracks and shaking the glass in the windows. I didn't enjoy the storm, but it was appropriate, the only contribution to our feeling that did not follow regulations or have a stamp of government control on it. Everything was suspended. We slept in our clothes. When the door to the dorm opened, we expected a man to enter with news—good or bad—which would guide actions and feelings.

I tried to recall the face of each man on the crew, even the officers, because I required sorrow from myself.

On the third day, the master-at-arms, a chief petty officer, came around to say that all hope for the aircraft was lost. The search we had never engaged in was being called off; the men were considered dead. He also told us that it would be a good idea to write home, quickly, for news of the missing airplane had reached the press; no names were given, but our squadron had been publicized.

"You know how them papers are at home," he said. "They want to scare people, to sell papers. If you don't want to cause your folks some real pain, write. I knew a guy who creamed in a helicopter, and he was saved, see, but the papers printed as how his outfit lost a ship, see, so his old lady, she was pregnant, she dropped the kid. You men ought to write, specially if anybody in your immediate family is sick, got a bad heart or something.

"The whole lash-up's got two days off," the chief added. "There'll be some kind of memorial service in the hangar

on Saturday, at oh nine hundred. All hands will be there,
in dress blues."

We climbed out of the flight suits, went off to the
showers, took out the stationery for letters home. In the
dorm it was silent and solemn. The men were dead. No
question now.

It was then that the sailors began to mourn.

We had all been forewarned. Pat and others swore they
would get drunk as hell if those guys weren't found. During the three days there had been ripping, spontaneous
curses from all of us, born less of sorrow than of the
sudden sense of our futility. One man, Frank Franconi,
said, "Guys dying really drive me nuts. I just fall apart."
Others confirmed this.

"Boy, if those guys are dead, old Frank will really be
hurt. He hates it when guys die."

Frankie was a short, fat man, extremely strong, with an
almost hairless, pale body, the color of white cheese, which
he displayed in states of nakedness or near-nakedness whenever weather or room temperature permitted. The steam
was left on during our days of anguish, and he wandered
about in his skivvies or bare. He had a single-cratered moon
for a belly, and he patted and soothed it when clad in
shorts. Naked he divided his affection between gut and
genitals.

He was the squadron banker. He loaned at two-for-one
rates, plagued those who didn't pay up every payday. A
welsher was under seige. I saw Frankie urinate on a man's
bunk one night, dousing blankets, pillow, and all, because
the man had returned only the principal on a ten-dollar
loan and was boasting that Frankie would have some trouble getting to him for the interest.

Frankie had a sexual cast which disturbed others, even his friends. He was an exhibitionist, and when he went after women in town, he went in to get his "knob polished." He brought back details of the fellatio, which he shared with the dorm. He was too kind and solicitous toward those tender sailors who often got into flight crews because the complement of gunners was not complete. They were usually unskilled and anxious to please. Frankie was first ordnanceman in his crew, and a good one. He schooled novices, advised them, befriended them. Sometimes he drank with one, and it was not unusual for Frankie, in a moment of drunken camaraderie, to suddenly clutch the sailor and kiss him on the cheek.

It was a mistake. Horror and abashment would come flooding into the boy's face. But Frankie was equal to anything. If any man in the squadron accused him of deviation, Frankie would fight and probably beat the man. That was refutation enough. If the sailor was just mad, but sensible enough to know Frankie could crush him, then Frankie would begin with one of those senseless boot-camp tirades.

"You little fuckin' greenhorn pukes. You people come around to a fightin' outfit, a real lash-up, so goddamn dumb you don't know your ass from last Friday. And they stick you in a Peter Baker Mike. You're a goddamn danger to your shipmates. You can't do nothin' and you don't know nothin'. You guys could kill us all. Do you know what it means to do a job that could kill your buddies if you screw it up? Do you?"

It would continue. The right bluster, intimidation, and rank-pulling. The kid's outrage would give way to a sense of worthlessness, of being a burden. I have seen them mumble apologies when Frankie finished. He was an expert.

That was the trouble. Frankie was good at his profession. He took excellent care of guns and turrets. He was able to fill in for others. In his spare time he had picked up the code, he could operate radar, he was checked out on the flight panel so that he could do the mech's job. His greatest achievement was his ability to fly the planes. Few enlisted men knew how to land and take off.

"In the old Navy, they figured that once in a while the pilots might get shot up. So they taught us how to fly. In them days wars were real."

My memory is cruel to Frankie, and I won't vouch for its accuracy or freedom from prejudice. Of the twenty-seven men in the dorm, probably a half-dozen were equally despicable and competent; we who criticized them were totally dependent on their skills. To challenge their authority would have required us to become sailors, full-time and devoted Navy men.

I suppose one of the reasons why the wake for the dead remains so vivid, seventeen years later, is that the Navy men failed completely to convince us that they were human.

It began the following morning when four or five men came back from mess hall and brought out their bottles. Good whisky could be purchased tax free at the NCO club. Men bought it and hid it in their lockers, used it for home entertainment and in preparation for a night ashore. When the drinking began, Frankie was still in bed. He moaned about the "poor little bastards." He called for a flunky to fetch his whisky.

He was a finicky sailor; his gear was always neat and his locker sacrosanct.

"Don't touch nothin' else. It's rolled up in my seabag, down by my shoes. I can tell if you mess anything else around. And roll the bag up and put it back where you found it."

The sailor obeyed.

Frankie rose on an elbow, uncapped and drank from the bottle, capped it, got back into his bunk and took the bottle in under the covers.

"Did you lock that locker?"

"Yes."

"Did he, Pat?"

Pat was among those seated at the table. "Yeah, it's locked."

Frankie stayed in bed until noon, drinking occasionally, calling crewmates to him. Kramer went over and listened to Frankie's scheme for single-engine practice.

"We're gonna shape up," Kramer said, imitating him. "We're gonna get so's we can empty that fuckin' tub of every piece of gear in two minutes. We won't let you boys cream in. Nobody in crew nine's gonna freeze his nuts in the Sea of Japan."

At the table others were passing bottles to their friends and taking drinks in exchange. As they began to feel their alcohol, they began to pay impromptu tributes to the dead men.

"When a bitchin' guy like Jim McCracken gets killed flyin', you know damn well the world ain't worth tin shit. That McCracken was one of the *best*. A real radioman. Jesus Christ. What a fuckin' good guy, goddamn. Wasn't he, Pat? Huh? Bill, you knew him. Wasn't he? Oh, shit. What a good guy."

From Frankie's bunk came frequent groans and the rasp of the bottle being opened. Frankie was up after the noon meal. He walked around the dorm, stark naked, bottle in hand. He said nothing at first. He paced about, his huge feet slapping the wood, sighing. He had a wide face and big black eyes and they were sad; they belonged in a Pietà. They turned away from people, looked longingly out the window, studied the floor, pierced the ceiling. He began tossing his head.

"The poor guys. Jesus, I can't stand it when guys get killed. The poor guys."

Out of respect for Frankie's legendary torment, the men at the table began to rise and stand in the path of his perambulations, pat him lightly on the shoulder, utter calming words.

"Ain't your fault, kid."

"Can't do nothin' about it."

Pat Fanning didn't rise and, since I liked him, I was pleased with that. But twice he called me over in descending stages of his drunkenness to reassure me that Frankie really meant what he said, what he was doing.

"I've seen him this way before. He just can't stand it. He really can't."

Frankie was crying before long. The bottle was not half empty, and he often paused in his pacing to force a drink on some bystander. He strolled, and suddenly tears popped out on his cheeks.

"Oh the poor sonsofbitches! Some of them nothin' but babies. And some, like Jimmie, real sailors, good men. What a rotten thing! It rips me up!"

Those were real tears, and they soon were streaming down his face, slicking the thick cheeks. He stopped walking and began a general tremble. His shoulders shook, his belly wobbled in opposition, his huge white butt swayed.

"Now he's really started."

I noticed then that the dorm had filled up: people from other crews were coming in, taking seats on the bunks of friends. A squadron tradition was being celebrated and the word had gone around.

Frankie began to scream curses at the aircraft, the squadron, the war, the Navy, the country. There was no smooth transition. The change was sudden and complete. His eyes narrowed to fierceness.

"They give 'em planes that ain't worth a damn, that spin out and stall and can't even land in four-foot swells. They load 'em up with gas that ain't nothin' but explosive, so the whole goddamn ship is one big bomb, and then send 'em out over freezin' water. They just killed those guys, just murdered 'em, that's all. They don't give a flyin' fuck. Because there's always more of us. Right? We ain't nothin'. Cheap help. We ain't shit. They can kill us off. They don't lose nothin'.

"They send us out in ass-freezin' weather in obsolete airplanes that ain't any good for anything. And the crews are loaded down with dead-beat punks who don't even know what a ship smells like. In the old days we were seamen first, airmen afterwards. We could tie and knot and throw a line. We were sailors."

No applause for that, not even from his peers.

He went through the sailor's plight. The bar owners that sucked up the monthly wage and wouldn't give you a free drink if you came at them with a belaying pin. ("You can sit there, smilin' at 'em, night after night, and they don't even know your last fuckin' name.") The used-car dealers who sold them junk machines. ("I bought one and the heap threw three rods in one hour after the warantee wore off.") The idea of trying to pick up women.

("The only ones you can look at without gettin' a gutful of whisky won't talk to you. Unless the bitches are married to a shipmate in the alternate squadron.") The treatment by civilians generally. He quoted a boot-camp adage: If a civilian, staggering drunk, fell in a gutter and covered himself with geysers of vomit, the civvies would say: "The poor man is sick." And if a sailor, chest covered with ribbons, twisted an ankle and stumbled while trying to save a child from rape by gangsters, the civvies would say: "Arrest that drunk."

Frankie was wet to the collarbone when he came around to his mother, and all the mothers whose sons were perishing in rotten ships with rotten pilots and crews made up of amateurs.

"Right now they're gettin' a knock on the door. Right now they're readin' those telegrams. Think of that. Good-fuckin-bye, son. Dead out here, froze or ruined."

He began to grope the air with his hands, a fat mime, holding the telegram. He tore it open, read it, and howled. Howled again and again, with a shrillness I'd never heard from animal or man before. I haven't heard it since.

It was the only time in his whole performance that I believed he was hurt. And he didn't give that time to sink in. In the midst of all his blubbering, he raised his eyes and crossed himself.

"May the Holy Father protect Mama from ever becoming a gold-star mother like the old ladies of all them poor bastards who died out there the other day."

His bottle was never emptied; there was always the suspicion that he was not drunk. But his stagger rapidly became dangerous. He would appear to lose balance on one side of the room; and in order to catch it, he would have to trot, knocking aside people and banging into lockers. He fell once against the edge of the table, cut his forehead so that blood gushed down into his eyebrow and along his nose and cheek. It smeared with his sweat, splattering throughout the barracks each time he jerked his head. He seemed not to notice the blood.

He asked for the names of the dead, many of whom he couldn't place.

"What did Joe Moody look like?"

"He was the little guy with glasses. He could sing."

"Oh, yeah, little Joe with the glasses. What a fine kid. Little guy, yeah. I know. Jesus, why should a little turd like that die? I mean, who'd he ever hurt?" He would shake his head and distribute the gore. "Who was the third mech?"

"That was Joe Moody, for God's sake."

"Oh, sure, sure. Little Joe Moody. I thought he was a metalsmith striker. Little Joe. Who the hell did *he* ever hurt?"

In the evening we went off to eat again. Frankie was once again in tears when we returned.

There were others asleep at the table or sprawled in their bunks. Pat Fanning and another mech were talking about Alaska. Once in a while Pat, alone among the career sailors, considered getting out when his hitch was up, going to Alaska to homestead. He spoke this way in spite of ten years' service and his ruined good looks.

"Sure," Frankie said. "Go to Alaska. But what about Jimmie McCracken? Ain't no Alaska for Jimmie McCracken."

Pat nodded, went over to Frankie, who was blubbering, and patted his shoulder.

"Poor Jimmie, huh? Poor Jimmie. Ain't that right?"

"Oh, yeah," Frankie wailed. "The poor shit."

It went on most of the night. Those who fell asleep revived later. There were sodden prayers uttered at impromptu funeral services, several thick tongues struggling through the intricacies of the Lord's Prayer. Someone sang a portion of the Navy hymn over and over.

A sober sailor screamed out for silence sometime after midnight, and all the mourners gathered at his bunk and threatened to turn him out.

"Get down, you prick, and we'll kill you! We'll kill *all* you punks who don't care when your buddies get killed! Wish to Christ that plane had been loaded with you cruds and we still had Jimmie McCracken with us."

"'Member how old Jimmie used to run his toothpaste test every mornin'?"

"Yeah. We'll never have another guy like Jimmie."

"Poor old Jimmie."

At nine the next morning the squadron met at the hangar, all sailors dressed in blues and wearing peacoats and winter hats. We lined up by crews. At the gap in the rank were thirteen small, hastily-prepared floral wreaths, unsteady on their bamboo tripods. Pinned to each was a hand-lettered card with the name, birth date, birthplace, rate or rank of the deceased. The storm had broken but the wind howled in through the hangar door, and two personnel men had to stand among the wreaths and keep them upright during the chaplain's talk.

He was a thick-necked, blond man, built like Frankie, with a curt, uncomfortable manner. He prayed once. Then he told us that these dead were good men and heroes.

That they died for a cause which had the support of God. That no man was free until all were free and those who perished in the struggle for freedom never really died.

The captain said the same thing.

There were almost two hundred men in that rusted tin barn on that cold morning. Their heads were bowed. Many of them had colds and were sniffing and snorting. But some were crying openly. Frankie Franconi was. And Pat Fanning.

The next night the captain's plane flew up the coast of Korea with all the wreaths piled in the after station. They were directed toward the general area of the watery grave of our shipmates by the command ship of the task force. The hatches were opened, and the wreaths were quickly dumped into the sea. No words were said. Enough had been said.

"There's a war to be fought," said the captain.